Degrassi Junior High:
Caitlin

Degrassi Junior High:
Caitlin

Catherine Dunphy

James Lorimer & Company Ltd., Publishers
Toronto

James Lorimer & Company Ltd. acknowledges the support of the Ontario Arts Council. We acknowledge the support of the Government of Canada through the Book Publishing Industry Development Program (BPIDP) for our publishing activities. We acknowledge the support of the Canada Council for the Arts for our publishing program. We acknowledge the support of the Government of Ontario through the Ontario Media Development Corporation's Ontario Book Initiative.

The Canada Council | Le Conseil des Arts
for the Arts | du Canada

ONTARIO ARTS COUNCIL
CONSEIL DES ARTS DE L'ONTARIO

Library and Archives Canada Cataloguing in Publication
Dunphy, Catherine, 1946-
    Degrassi Junior High : Caitlin / by Catherine Dunphy.
Based on characters and stories from the television series Degrassi Junior High.
Previously published as: Caitlin, 1990.
ISBN-13: 978-1-55028-923-7 ISBN-10: 1-55028-923-3
    I. Title. II. Title: Caitlin.
PS8557.U554C34 2006   jC813'.54   C2006-901480-9

This book is based on characters and stories from the television series Degrassi Junior High, created by Linda Schuyler and Kit Hood for Playing With Time Inc., with Yan Moore as supervising writer. Playing With Time Inc. acknowledges with thanks the writers — Yan Moore, Avrum Jacobson, Susin Nielsen, Kathryn Ellis — whose enthusiasm and dedication helped produce the original scripts upon which this original story by Catherine Dunphy is based.

James Lorimer & Company Ltd.,
Publishers
317 Adelaide Street West, Suite 1002
Toronto, Ontario
M5V 1P9
www.lorimer.ca
Printed and bound in Canada

Distributed in the
U.S. by:
Orca Book Publishers
P.O. Box 468
Custer, WA USA
98240

1

His jaw clenched, Mr. Raditch pointed to the two girls.

"That's quite enough," he snapped, his voice pitched dangerously low.

Kathleen fell silent. Caitlin froze. She felt a shiver go up her back. She'd blown it, she knew it. She couldn't meet Mr. Raditch's angry eyes.

"What kind of behaviour is this?" he growled at both girls. "You two know better than to bring your past quarrels to a *Digest* meeting. I trust you won't do it again. The rest of us do not wish to be subjected to any more of your childish squabbles. Have I made myself perfectly clear?"

"I just want to know why she's blocking my article." Kathleen pursed her lips and stuck out her chin.

The grade eight teacher ignored her.

"Caitlin?" he said sternly.

Caitlin looked down at her fidgeting hands. Her throat was dry, like she was about to cry. The words wouldn't come.

She could hear Trish twist around in the seat next to her. The red-haired girl reached under the battered wooden table for Caitlin's hand and squeezed it.

Good old Trish, Caitlin thought, giving her assistant editor a quick grateful look.

Sometimes she wondered whether they would even have a school newspaper if it weren't for Trish. Efficient, always smiling, a hard worker, and loyal. Yeah, loyal to the end, which was now.

Caitlin waited for the next words from Mr. Raditch. He was going to fire her — she just knew it.

She knew what he was going to say: "I'm sorry, Caitlin, having you as editor of the school newspaper is just not working out."

Everything she had ever wanted — to be editor of the *Digest,* to write articles on important topics, to try to make things better in the world — was ending right now.

"I'm sorry for the interruption," Mr. Raditch was saying. "Let's get back to matters at hand. Kathleen, we will run your story on why Degrassi should have a dress code. But I agree with Caitlin. It should not be on the front page."

Caitlin's head shot up. She'd won. She'd won. Kathleen glared at her through narrowed eyes.

"But," Mr. Raditch continued, "I don't believe Caitlin's story about the chemicals in our drinking water is front-page material either. It's not the kind of story we want in every issue of the *Digest*. We need to have a good mix."

"But this is important," Caitlin blurted. She sounded weak, whiney, but she couldn't stop herself. Being *Digest* editor was all she had ever wanted and now, after just two editions, Mr. Raditch was taking over, taking the decisions away from her and the staff.

The door to the crowded newspaper office suddenly flew open, banging with a loud thud against the bookcase next to the wall.

"Hey, guys, stop the presses. Have I got hot news for you." Joey Jeremiah stood in the doorway, skateboard in hand, hat on head and a big grin on his face. It started to fade as he looked around the table and saw everybody's faces.

"He-e-y, it can wait," he said, backing out the door. "Another time. No problem, man."

"Stay, Joey." Mr. Raditch stopped him. "I want the others to hear your news." The teacher sounded calm. "I asked Joey to drop by today because I wanted him to tell you himself. Then I want us to do a little brainstorming."

Caitlin drew a deep breath and fought to get a grip on herself. She was not going to let Mr. Raditch see how upset she was. Not Joey Jeremiah, either.

Joey's bright brown eyes went from Mr. Raditch to Caitlin, then back to the teacher. With a puzzled frown, he dropped into the chair across the table from Kathleen. The room went quiet as everybody turned and looked at him.

"Well, um, the news is that we have Murray Cram for the dance," he said, keeping his eyes downcast.

Trish let out a whoop. "You mean the guy on CRA-Z?"

"Wow! How'd you ever get him?" asked Diana. She helped Trish print and collate the paper. The *Digest* was the only thing Diana's Greek-born parents let her do. They were very strict and refused to let her go to school dances, even though she loved music and was always listening to the radio in the *Digest* office.

Joey grinned. This was the reaction he had been hoping for. "The same," he said, leaning back on the chair and pushing his hat to the back of his head. "He's my man. He said he'd do it for me."

"Sure, Joey." Kathleen sounded disgusted. "The most popular deejay in town is your best friend. And I hang out with Madonna."

"Well, I do know him a little." The front legs of Joey's chair hit the floor with a bang and the cocky grin faded from the boy's face. "Remember the Battle of the Bands last summer? The one we almost won? One of the judges was a friend of Murray's."

"The point being," Mr. Raditch broke in, "that Degrassi is pretty darn fortunate to have Murray Cram host our dance. What other school can claim that?"

Caitlin shot a surprised look at the teacher. He looked as pleased as Joey. *So this is what he cares about*, she thought, *not the quality of the water we drink*.

"We're going to make this the best dance Degrassi has ever had," the young, intense English teacher continued.

"And we are going to make enough money to send all the grade eights on a field trip to Washington next Easter. This is where the *Digest* comes in. We're going to make sure everyone in the school buys a ticket for the dance."

He bent down and unlocked his briefcase. "And we're going to make sure everyone buys one of these."

He held up a large royal-blue sweatshirt with two words — *Degrassi Digest* — scrawled in white across the entire front. "This is our next front page," he said in a proud voice.

"All right." Joey punched the air with his fist. Caitlin looked around the room. Trish and Diana were grinning, and even Kathleen looked impressed. Everybody loved the idea — everybody but her.

"That's the front page?" she asked. She couldn't keep the scorn out of her voice.

Joey darted a look at the teacher. His chair scraped against the floor as he jumped up and pushed it away.

"So, uh, great ... the dance, I mean," he said, heading for the door. "Gotta go. I'm outta here."

The other students looked longingly at the door.

"That's enough for today's meeting," Mr. Raditch said quietly but firmly. He looked stern. "I'd like Caitlin to stay for a moment, but the rest of you can go."

Kathleen waltzed past Caitlin, smirking. Trish, quickly collecting her books and notes, gave Caitlin one woebegone look as she scurried out with Diana.

Caitlin twisted a strand of her brown hair. She, Caitlin Ryan, straight-A student, was in serious trouble. Maybe she shouldn't have refused to run Kathleen's stupid story about why school uniforms were a good idea, even though there was room for only one more story in this month's *Digest* and she knew hers was more important.

Mr. Raditch must have been reading her mind. "We agree about one thing," he was saying. "Having a clean water supply is more important than school uniforms."

He ran a hand through his thick hair, stretched his arms back over his head, and then leaned over the table towards her. He wasn't angry, she realized; he looked plain tired.

"The thing about papers — all papers, ours too — is you've got to have a lot of stories about a lot of different things. Things that someone bright and intelligent like you might not think are much, but that other people care about." He looked straight at her. "That's the tough part about putting out a paper, getting the balance down. But you'll pick it up pretty soon. You've got the writing part of it down to a fine art now."

Caitlin felt her face flush with pleasure.

"Thanks, Mr. Raditch," she said, and smiled at him.

But the teacher was frowning at the *Digest* deadline schedule in front of him. He tapped the piece of paper with a pencil. "The issue is due out next Wednesday," he said, "so you've got until the end of this week to write the story about Murray Cram."

He wanted her to write the story? Caitlin couldn't believe it. She stared at him, speechless

Mr. Raditch was packing up his briefcase. He didn't see the look on her face. "It's not the front page, though. I think that should be the sweatshirt. It'll be dramatic, eh? Make the *Digest* look like a professional magazine."

"No story on the front?" Caitlin couldn't stop herself from saying.

"Not this time. It'll make a nice change," the teacher replied. He sounded casual, but he was watching her reaction intently.

Caitlin took a deep breath. "I think we should always have a good story on the front page," she said. Her voice trembled with fear. Here she was fighting — again — with a teacher. But she forced herself go on. "It is a newspaper. It shouldn't be used as a — a — " she searched her mind for just the right word " — an advertising flyer making kids spend their money."

She had gone too far. Mr. Raditch clenched his closed briefcase so hard his knuckles were white. She watched him fight to keep his temper under control.

After what seemed like minutes but was probably just a few seconds, he slowly uncurled himself from the rickety wooden chair and walked deliberately to the door. With one hand on the door, he turned and said in a calm and reasonable voice, "Caitlin, you are getting carried away. You know that is not what I see for the future of the

Digest. You know the trip to Washington is important, but promoting morale within the school is not trivial either."

"So, for this issue," his pale grey eyes bored into hers, "that's *this* issue, not the next one and not the one after that, the December *Digest* will have a picture of the new school sweatshirt on the front page. Inside will be a story about it, written by our best journalist."

Mr. Raditch's face softened. "That's you, by the way. You'll have the story on my desk by Friday?"

Caitlin nodded miserably, her fire doused by his unchanging position.

The teacher opened the door. "Good. That's settled then. Want a lift anywhere?"

Caitlin's head jerked up in surprise. "No. Thanks."

When the door closed behind him, she slumped back in her hard seat. Write about a dance and a stupid sweatshirt. She might as well write commercials. This wasn't what she wanted to do. This wasn't the way her life was supposed to be.

She picked up her books and slowly walked out of the deserted school. On the front steps she paused and took a deep breath of the crisp fall air. It wasn't fair; it just wasn't fair. She wanted to scream the words at the top of her lungs, again and again.

Instead, in a sudden burst, she ran down the steps into the street, not looking back. She had to get away from there, from everything.

2

A car rounding the corner on two screeching wheels and leaving behind the acrid smell of burning rubber brought Caitlin to a halt. Gasping for breath, she backed onto the sidewalk, staring dumbly after the speeding car that had cut off her flight.

What was her hurry, anyway? She had no place to go.

She kicked the leaves off the sidewalk and watched them fly up, then swirl back down to her feet. She shivered in the cool November air and shoved her hands in the pockets of her duffle coat.

She could forget about her dreams of making the *Digest* a really good newspaper.

What could she about it? Absolutely nothing. Well, she could quit, but what good would that do? She wanted to be editor, even if it meant having her name on something she wasn't very proud of. Caitlin sighed at the thought.

She wasn't going to quit, she knew that. She wasn't the type.

No way. Her type always stuck it out. Her type went home, took a deep breath, held her nose and wrote the stupid story about the stupid dance. And her type handed it in — early — on Mr. Raditch's desk.

"Might as well get it over with," she told herself as she turned and headed for home.

Her mother was at the kitchen table again, working. She didn't look up when Caitlin came in, just muttered, "Caitlin, I've got so much work to finish tonight, I'll be at it forever."

"How was my day? Awful, but thanks for asking," Caitlin said to herself as she hung her coat in the hallway. She came back to the kitchen and peered over her mother's tense shoulder. "What's that? Oh-h. You gave them a surprise history quiz. They must have loved you."

"These kids don't realize it's more work for me. It's not as if I don't have other things to do. I have to work out a staff timetable for lunchroom duty. There's so many kids being bussed into the school now, we've got to organize lunch time supervision. And there's a home-and-school meeting next week. But, no, first I have to read and mark their feeble efforts," Mrs. Ryan said grimly.

Caitlin looked at her mother. Never before had she heard her say mean things about the kids she taught. But this was her first year as a public school vice-principal, and she was very stressed.

Caitlin bit her lip. Not a great time to tell her mom

about her own *Digest* troubles. With a sigh, she took a tray of pork chops out of the refrigerator.

"Dad home for dinner tonight?" she asked.

"No," her mother snapped.

Since her mother had started her new job, Caitlin's dad was spending more time at his tennis club. He said he was trying to get in shape and give her mother some time to herself, but Caitlin missed him.

With another sigh, she put the chops in the oven, crept to the dining room to set the table, then went to her room to write up the thrilling news about Murray Cram.

"He wants it by the end of the week — he shall have it tomorrow," she said to herself through clenched teeth as she read back the screen she'd filled on her computer.

> Degrassi's got a new dress code, and for once, there are no complaints. This is one sweat that takes the sweat out of what to wear. And you can order yours only at the year's biggest and best star-studded dance. Star-studded, you sneer? Oh yeah?
>
> Oh yeah! Spinning the vinyl from his personal record collection is none other than the wildest, funniest man on radio, CRA-Z's Murray Cram.

Caitlin made a face. Maybe she had overdone it a little.

Didn't matter. It was done, she told herself as she made a printout of the story and headed back downstairs.

She cut some raw vegetables and arranged them on plates with the chops.

"Mom," she said quietly. "Dinner. It's ready."

Mrs. Ryan didn't look up from her papers. "I don't have time for food," she said in a tight voice. "Just throw the plate down here."

"Don't tempt me," Caitlin said before she could stop herself.

Her mother slowly put down her marking pencil.

"This is hard on you, isn't it?" she asked.

Caitlin felt tears well in her eyes and turned away, but not quickly enough. Her mother pushed her papers in an untidy heap to one side of the kitchen table. She stood up, walked over to Caitlin, and squeezed her dejected shoulders. Then she picked up both plates and carried them back to the table.

"Come sit with me," she said.

Reluctantly Caitlin dropped into her place at the table. "I'm not hungry," she said.

Her mother reached for the salt and pepper. "We haven't done much together lately," she said. "We haven't had our Saturday bargain hunt lately, have we? We haven't been to a movie in a while either." She made a face and tried to joke with Caitlin. "No wonder we're no fun. We haven't had any fun."

When Caitlin wouldn't smile or answer, Mrs. Ryan dropped her jolly tone of voice. She leaned over the table, tapping Caitlin's untouched plate of food with her fork, and said, "I've just realized something. You haven't had any friends over this year yet, have you? Is it because of me and all my work?"

"No, that's not it, at least not all of it," Caitlin replied. There was no point trying to fool herself or lie to her mother. She hadn't had any friends over because she didn't have any friends anymore. Not since Susie. Ever since her best friend had moved, Caitlin had felt like part of her had left, too. All last year she and Susie had planned what they were going to do when they were in grade eight, at the top of Degrassi. They were going to run the school

Caitlin sighed. Susie was going to be president of the student council and she was going to take over the *Digest* and make it really say things.

But the dream ended that day last summer by the pool.

It had been so hot, everything seemed to be shimmering. It was so humid that the air felt like a heavy blanket. Caitlin didn't even think she had enough energy to roll over to tan her back.

"I'm going to be like a piece of toast — burnt on one side," she said with a happy groan to Susie lying next to her.

Susie stretched out her legs, wiggled her toes, and groaned back. But Kathleen flopped and fidgeted and fussed. Finally she picked up her towel and stood over the girls, blocking the sun. "Don't you know that too much tanning causes skin cancer? I'm going over to the shade."

Caitlin shielded her eyes with her hand and watched Kathleen's tall pale form as the girl picked her way through the other bathers lying in the sun. She watched Kathleen spread out her towel in the shadow of the change building. Trust her to take the fun out of the day. But she was right about tanning and skin cancer. Caitlin looked down at her slim legs and arms. She was lucky she had the kind of skin that tanned easily; she was turning a nice golden-brown already.

Susie rolled over on her back. "Is she gone?" she mumbled into her scrunched-up towel. "Good. Who asked her along, anyway?"

Caitlin sat up and slipped on a T-shirt. "You did, remember?" she grinned, poking her buddy in the arm. "I think I should go in now, anyway, otherwise I will burn," she said, glancing at Susie's smooth brown skin. "That's something you don't have to worry about."

She expected Susie's usual "Hey, black is beautiful, right?" but her friend was quiet.

Caitlin scrambled off her towel, stood up, and stretched. She turned back to Susie, who still lay with her eyes closed. "Coming?" she asked. "I'm buying the ice cream."

"Caitlin, I'm moving," Susie said softly.

Caitlin suddenly felt weak. "Where to?"

"Markham. They've bought a bigger house. New. My mom loves it. It's only a fifty-minute drive from Degrassi, that's what my dad says, but my mom says it's more like an hour and a half the way other people drive." Susie tried to laugh, but she didn't look at Caitlin.

"Well, I guess I'll see for myself when I get a licence." Caitlin tried to laugh too.

She dropped back on the ground, her legs weak at the knees, like a rag doll's. Grade eight without Susie? Degrassi without Susie Rivera, vice-president of the student council?

Kathleen came back, snapping her beach towel. "I'm starving," she said. "Let's get something to eat."

Seeing them just sitting, she pursed her lips and put one hand on her hip.

"What's the matter with you two? You look as if you'd lost your best friend," she said.

Caitlin and Susie just looked at each other. They had.

Caitlin looked down at the kitchen table. She still missed Susie. Every day. At first Susie had stayed weekends with Caitlin a lot, but lately she was getting busier at her new school and making new friends.

Caitlin sighed. New friends. Susie was lucky.

"How about a pajama party? Ask some girls over for this Friday. Come on, you'll have fun," Caitlin's mother urged her.

Pajama party? Caitlin managed a weak smile for her

mother, but inside she fretted. Who was she supposed to ask? Besides Susie, that is. Kathleen? Last year they had sort of been friends, but not this year since the fight about the *Digest* articles. Trish? Trish was only in grade seven. Melanie? Caitlin frowned a little, then her face cleared. Maybe Melanie.

"Caitlin, wa-a-a-ait up."

Even through Tanita Tikaram's smokey voice in her headset, Caitlin could hear what sounded like her name being called. Probably the wind.

She checked her notebook — the story on the dance and sweatshirt was still there — and quickened her pace. The sooner she got to school, the sooner she could turn it in, and the sooner it would be out of her life.

"Caitlin, slow down, for crying out loud." It was Melanie, face flushed, gasping from running.

Caitlin removed her earphones. So she *had* heard her name being called. She was getting too used to being alone.

"Hi, Melanie." She smiled at the tall girl whose straight brown hair was being blown across her face by the wind.

Melanie peered at Caitlin. "How'd you get your hair like that? Mine always falls out."

Caitlin had pulled her hair into a thick French braid and then tied it with a leopard-print scarf she had found in a secondhand clothing store. Today she had put on a matching leopard-print cinch belt over her black dress. She liked pulling things together — especially those cheap fashion finds she and her mom used to go out scouting for — but she'd never realized before that anyone ever noticed.

"Thanks," Caitlin said. "What's new with you?"

Melanie grinned and shook her hair out of her face. "Snake called last night," she said.

Melanie had it bad for Snake. She'd had a crush on him ever since she first heard him play in the Zit Remedy — Joey's band — last year. "He's asked me to the dance."

The dance. Caitlin wanted to groan. Still, she envied Melanie.

"That's great. You're really lucky," she told her. And she meant it.

"Why don't you and Joey come along with us?" Melanie chattered, not noticing how Caitlin shivered at the words.

Caitlin couldn't imagine spending a whole evening with a boy. What would they talk about? And Joey? Just because he had asked her to a dance last year didn't mean she had a crush on him. But Caitlin had to admit that of all the boys she knew, Joey was the one who was always laughing or joking around. At least there wouldn't be any of those awful silences.

"I don't think Joey wants to go anywhere with me." She pulled a face. "Joey's hot; I just get red in the face. Joey's cool; I'm plain cold. Joey thinks he's hip; I know I'm zip."

Melanie laughed, then she stared at Caitlin. "Come on, don't put yourself down. You don't mean that. Besides, that's almost good enough to be a rap."

"*Almost* is the important word there," Caitlin retorted with a groan.

The bell rang as they hurried up the school steps.

"Don't be too sure Joey doesn't want to go places with you," Melanie hissed as they slid into their seats in Mr. Raditch's class.

Caitlin didn't answer. She was on her way to the teacher's desk to drop off the article when Mr. Raditch burst into the classroom.

"Good morning," he called from the back of the room. It was a warning, not a greeting. He strode to the front of the room, removing Joey's hat in one practised motion without breaking stride. He glanced at the paper Caitlin had left on his desk, and nodded at her.

"This morning we're starting on something a little different." He snapped open his briefcase, took out a sheaf of paper, and sat on the edge of his desk facing the class.

"I've taken it upon myself to assign study partners. A few of our less, uh, motivated students are already falling behind. So before we get any further in the year I want to put a stop to this. Each set of partners will meet once a week on Tuesdays, either before or after school, before or after dinner" — Mr. Raditch paused as a titter spread throughout the class — "to work together on certain assignments. Now, I've picked Tuesday because I've checked. There are no football practices that day, no meetings of the camera club or the drama club and therefore there are no excuses. Have I made myself clear?"

Several of the students in the front of the rows nodded automatically.

"Good," the teacher continued. "I've paired up people according to what subjects need some working on." He cleared his throat. "Let me make it clear this is not a popularity contest. This is hard work and this is mandatory."

"Awwww, no way," Joey groaned loudly, sliding down in his chair.

"Oh, yes," Mr. Raditch replied. "In fact, Mr. Jeremiah, it is for students such as yourself that I've organized these pairings. I've put you with Caitlin. I think you can learn a lot from her about proper work habits, getting work done on time, if not ahead of time, and doing it well."

"Awww, man," Joey wailed. He glared at his desk.

From the back of the room, Caitlin could hear Kathleen titter. "Poor Joey, that's awful to have to study with Caitlin," she sneered in a voice loud enough to carry to the four corners of the classroom.

The boys hooted as Mr. Raditch called for order.

Caitlin's face burned. The whole class now knew what Joey thought of her.

3

Caitlin slammed her locker door.

She slipped on her earphones and turned up the volume. She'd done it. Melanie was coming to the pajama party. So was Kathleen. She would call Susie tonight. At least her mother would be happy.

Melanie wanted her favourite movie for the party — *Dirty Dancing*. She might as well drop by the video store and reserve it before she went home.

"You listening to us?"

Caitlin froze. It was Joey, blocking her way to the front door. He was smiling.

Caitlin didn't smile back. Inside she was exploding with rage. After what he did to her in front of the whole class, he thought he could be nice to her now? He must really take her for a fool.

"Is that our tape?" he repeated.

"No," Caitlin said angrily and tried to push by him.

Last year she had bought one of the two-dollar copies

of the Zit Remedy tape Joey had sold. But that was last year. This year she wanted to go home and cut it into a thousand little pieces.

"Hey, what's the rush?" Joey said, staggering back a few steps. "We've got to work out when we study together."

Caitlin glared. "Forget it. You don't want to study with me. That's obvious."

A look of panic crossed Joey's face.

"You're not going to do it then?" he asked in a small voice. All the bluster had gone out of him.

"No way," Caitlin snorted. "Study yourself."

"Caitlin, I don't want to fail again," Joey said, turning his face away from her.

The anger in her died down. He looked sad. And scared.

It must be awful to worry about failing. He was the only one in the school who had to repeat grade eight. All his friends — like Snake and Wheels — were in grade nine now.

Maybe what he did in class today was because he was embarrassed he needed help. Maybe it wasn't because she was his partner. Maybe.

Caitlin looked at Joey. "We could meet Mondays after school in the library," she said.

"We could?" Joey gasped. "But Mr. Raditch said Tues — I mean, great. Okay, it's a date."

He fell into step beside her. At the street, he stopped.

Why didn't he leave? Caitlin squirmed. She couldn't think of anything more to talk about.

"So," Joey cleared his throat. "You going to the dance?" Caitlin felt her face reddening.

"Maybe. I don't know," she sputtered.

"Aww, you've gotta go. C'mon, I want you to go. What do you say? I'll see you there. Okay?" Joey winked and clattered away on his skateboard.

In spite of herself, Caitlin smiled. She walked slowly to the video store, lost in thought. So, had she finally got a date? She shook her head. It was best not to get carried away by anything Joey said. Not yet anyway, she thought, as she reached the video store.

Only one other person was in The Big Seen, and that woman was just leaving. She held the door open for Caitlin. The clerk was at the counter watching something on the television. His back was turned to her. Politely Caitlin waited, shifting from one foot to another. He must have known she was there, but still he watched the television.

"Excuse me, can I reserve a movie for Friday?" she finally asked.

"Has it got a name?" the clerk answered, not turning away from the TV.

Caitlin stopped shifting. This guy was rude. She glared at his back, not answering.

She watched him reach up and push the pause button.

It took so long he looked as if he was in slow motion. Then he turned around and picked up a pen.

"Name?" he grunted, not looking up.

For the second time in a hour, Caitlin was swimming in anger. It was so strong she couldn't say a word. She could only glare.

The clerk must have felt her waves of fury. Finally looking at her, he cleared his throat and said gruffly but with none of the rudeness of before, "I need a name for the order form."

"Caitlin Ryan."

He smirked. His sleek dark-brown hair was held in a ponytail by a rubber band. The sleeves of his denim work shirt were rolled up showing strong, muscular arms. He wore a vest made of leather the colour of melted butter-scotch. His startling blue eyes were framed by thick dark lashes any girl would envy. But he didn't look friendly. His cool eyes slid over Caitlin, taking in her trim black dress, leopard skin belt and scarf. Then a small smile played at the corner of his mouth. He met her eyes and said: "I meant, name of the movie."

Caitlin blushed. How could she be so stupid?

"*Dirty Dancing*," she said meekly, suddenly embarrassed and wishing it were another movie, any other movie.

She heard him mutter "garbage" under his breath as he wrote it down and got the spelling of her name. He turned back to the television set and pushed the start button.

Caitlin knew she was dismissed, but she stood there. On the screen, a dark-haired woman in a red dress was speaking to a group in an auditorium. Probably university students.

"You are all children of the atomic age," she was saying in a strange accent. Not English, but not unlike it. "You have grown up with this. Some of you are probably having nightmares about nuclear war."

Caitlin leaned forward over the counter.

"Today America has 30,000 to 35,000 nuclear weapons. That's enough, they say, the Pentagon says, to overkill — which is a Pentagon word and not a medical term — every Russian human being forty times. Russia has 20,000 bombs. That's enough to overkill every American human being twenty times. So who's ahead and who's behind?"

Caitlin forgot she didn't like this clerk. "Excuse me," she said, "What movie is that? Who is she?"

"Why do you want to know?" he said, but he didn't sound angry. He turned off the video, pushed rewind and for the first time looked straight into her eyes. He was either eighteen or nineteen and, Caitlin noticed, very good-looking, with a straight nose and square jaw. He looked as if he didn't smile very often.

"It's what she's saying. It's so right. It's so stupid, bombs and killing people. What does overkilling mean, anyway? Dead is dead, right?"

"Don't ask me. Ask the Pentagon, the Americans. It's their word."

Caitlin was too worked up to stop.

"Overkill, what kind of a word is that?" she said indignantly. "And these are the people who are running our world? Making all the decisions about bombs and nuclear missiles? That's just terrific. Why isn't somebody doing something to stop this?"

The clerk was staring at her, listening hard. "You into this stuff?" he asked.

"Of course I am," Caitlin said. Her hands curled into fists and she shoved them into her pockets. What a question.

He slid the tape into its jacket and handed it to her.

"Here," he said. "Take it."

Caitlin reached for her purse.

"It's free," he said.

"Why?" Caitlin blurted.

"Because you don't giggle." He ducked under the counter and handed her another video. "Might as well take this one now. Have 'em both back Saturday."

Caitlin looked at the cassettes in her hand. *Dirty Dancing*. And something called *If You Love This Planet*.

"Thanks," she called out as the clerk vaulted over the counter and disappeared into a storeroom.

4

She was here. At last. Walking through the front door, grinning just the way she used to when she had pulled off another A.

"Susie," Caitlin squealed, running towards her friend, her best friend. Then she stopped. "Oh, your hair's great."

"Like it? It's the new me," said Susie with a wave of her hand. "I figured I had to do something to make these Markham kids notice that there's a new girl in town." She grinned. "And they've noticed, all right."

She strutted through the front hall, showing off her new look. She had cut her curls and shaved her hair close to her head on the sides. It looked a bit like a Grace Jones, only prettier, Caitlin thought, staring at her friend.

It wasn't that Susie didn't look great — just kind of different. Older maybe. Caitlin frowned. She had thrown on a big old black sweatshirt, but Susie was wearing black jodhpurs that looked really expensive, knee-high leather boots, and a billowing creamy white silk shirt.

Boy, you don't see someone for two months and everything changes, Caitlin thought.

Mr. Ryan was hanging up Susie's coat, but he must have caught his daughter's frown.

"Don't worry, sweetie. It's the same old Susie, just new hair," he whispered to her as he walked past them into the kitchen.

Caitlin straightened her shoulders. Of course. Her dad was right. She was beginning to doubt everything lately. She had two hours alone with her best friend before Kathleen and Melanie arrived for pizza, movies, and the sleepover. She'd better make the most of it.

"Come on, let's take your things upstairs to my room," she said.

Susie grinned. "And let's talk. I want to know everything that's been going on. Everything."

Caitlin raised an eyebrow. "No way I tell you everything, Susie Rivera. These are state secrets. You could blab them all over Markham."

"Hey, no fair. Talk or I'll pry it out of Kathleen and Melanie," Susie pretended to wring Caitlin's neck.

They burst out laughing and raced upstairs.

"You should see Joey. He's always watching her," Melanie said to Susie.

"Yeah, I hear. He's asked her to the dance, right?"

Caitlin grimaced. She knew she shouldn't have told

Susie what Joey had said about seeing her at the dance.

"Caitlin," Melanie wailed, "why didn't you tell me? We can go together. You and Joey. Me and Snake."

Caitlin could have killed herself. She wished she'd never told Susie. "It's not the same thing as you and Snake. He just said he'd see me there," she stammered.

Melanie interrupted her. "Joey likes you, Caitlin, come on. He watches you a lot in class."

"He's always at your locker. Don't forget that," said Kathleen.

"I have to be Joey's study partner, that's all," Caitlin explained to Susie. "He's pretty hopeless at French and math."

Susie made her mouth hang open on purpose. "Joey. Joey Jeremiah. The short guy with the dumb shirts and the skateboard? Joey F-for-Flirt Jeremiah? That one?"

"That one," said Melanie and Kathleen together.

"Except it's Joey F-for-Flunk Jeremiah," Kathleen added. "He's in our class now and he's still a pain in the ... class."

The girls collapsed in giggles.

"Let's watch the movie," Caitlin said, eager to change the topic.

The others ignored her.

"How's the swim team doing this year?" Susie asked Melanie.

"Rotten without you," was the answer. "You should

have seen what happened at the meet with Lakefront. A Degrassi di-sas-ter. Lakefront, they won everything, everything, plus the relay."

The girls subsided into silence, remembering the humiliating school defeat.

"Eyes front," Caitlin ordered her friends. "Ready for movies? Got everything?"

"Wait, wait." There was a scramble as they all grabbed pillows and blankets, and dove for the best places on the couch or settled on the floor.

"Hey, move the chips closer to me, will you?" Susie demanded as Caitlin turned on the VCR.

Here's hoping this works, she thought. *I hope they'll want to see it as much as I do.*

Caitlin had read the video jacket and knew the woman was Dr. Helen Caldicott, an Australian who had lectured all over the world against nuclear arms.

Caitlin looked at her three friends. *Please let them like it. Please let them care as much as me*, she thought. *Maybe if we all got together ....*

The profile of Helen Caldicott filled the screen. "So let's start at the beginning of the nuclear age," she was saying to the college students in the audience. "That was founded by Einstein, of course, when he discovered $E=MC^2$, energy equals the mass of the atom by the speed of light squared."

Melanie groaned. "This isn't *Dirty Dancing*."

"That's next. This is one I want you to see. It's short." Caitlin bit her lip. This probably wasn't going to work. It wasn't the right time or place to show this kind of movie, but if they could just listen to what Helen Caldicott was saying ....

"And Einstein said, The splitting of the atom has changed everything save man's mode of thinking. Thus we drift towards unparallelled catastrophe.'"

"I know her," Kathleen said suddenly.

"Well, I know who she sounds like," interrupted Susie. "Crocodile Dundee. Right, mate?"

"Come on, guys, give this a chance," Caitlin pleaded. "Look, there's Ronald Reagan when he was an actor."

The former president of the United States was being some goofy guy in the air force who wanted to be given a chance to blow up the enemy.

Susie started to giggle but she looked bored when Helen Caldicott came back on the screen: "One hydrogen bomb is four times the size of all the bombs dropped in World War II."

"Boo-o-o," said Melanie. "I want Patrick Swayze, not her, whoever she is."

"She's this woman who's a doctor and who goes all over the world talking about how we're all going to die," said Kathleen. "Caitlin, I really don't think we need to see this. Besides, I don't believe what she says will happen, not now that the Russians are into peace and being friendly with the West and even letting a McDonald's restaurant open in Moscow."

Caitlin was exasperated. "Kathleen, the Soviet Union still has lots of nuclear warheads. Don't be fooled. So do other countries. Like Libya. Anything could happen. We could still be blown up."

"Well, not before I get to go to a dance with Snake," said Melanie.

Susie threw a pillow at her. Melanie threw it back. They were shrieking at each other. Kathleen was smiling at the two of them.

Caitlin got up and quietly turned off the movie. *Dirty Dancing* it would be.

Later that night, when all the others were fast asleep, Caitlin lay awake. She could hear the soft breathing of her three friends sleeping near her. Susie was beside her on the pullout couch, Melanie had stretched out her long frame on the other couch, and Kathleen was on the floor. She said she needed strong support for her back.

Caitlin could reach out and practically touch all three of them, but she felt very alone. For a long time she lay there, not moving much, just thinking.

Then, finally she, too, fell asleep.

Caitlin half-heartedly shook the chip crumbs out of the cushions before flopping down on the couch.

Her friends had left half an hour ago, Melanie and

Kathleen to their homes and Susie back to Markham to meet some new friends at the mall.

The videos. Caitlin sat straight up. She had promised that guy in the store she would have them back that afternoon. What had she done with the other movie? Frantically she scoured the room. There it was, under the television listings magazine. Quickly she put it on.

The screen filled with the trademark of the National Film Board. Caitlin was surprised. *If You Love This Planet* was a Canadian movie.

The camera was slowly moving over the burned body of a boy caught in Hiroshima when the Americans dropped the atom bomb. Caitlin shuddered. He looked horrible. The burns seemed to be still raw.

The Australian woman was calmly reciting statistics: Some experts figure that ninety per cent of Americans will be dead ninety days after a nuclear war. They will die horribly. Canadians, too, she makes a point of saying.

Caitlin felt panic churn inside her, worse than anything she had felt before an exam.

If we have a nuclear war, the people left alive will envy those who are dead, Caldicott continued.

Caitlin hugged her knees tightly. She closed her eyes and could see the mushroom cloud of the Atomic bomb rising up over Toronto, just the way it had over that Japanese city. Beautiful, glowing, evil.

She rubbed her forehead against her knees. She was too

frightened to move. Caitlin was disgusted by herself. The woman in the movie — Helen Caldicott — was no wimp. She was a fighter. She wouldn't be clinging to a couch. *I want to be like her,* Caitlin thought, getting the tape and heading for the door. But the Big Seen was packed with people wanting a movie for Saturday night. The pony-tailed clerk was busy at the cash register and didn't look up as she walked in. Caitlin's shoulders slumped in disappointment. She had wanted to talk to him.

She placed the pair of videos near him on the counter.

"Here you are," she said quietly and turned towards the door. He looked up. "Caitlin, come by Monday, okay?" he said, waving the Caldicott video at her.

Caitlin felt her heart race. *He remembered my name,* she thought, *he remembered my name.*

5

Caitlin was the first one out the classroom door when school ended Monday. *Take it easy*, she told herself, *he'll be there*.

She fumbled her lock, jamming it.

"Wow, I've got it bad," she muttered, making herself slow down and dial her lock combination carefully this time. The door swung open, flattening Joey against the bank of neighbouring lockers.

"Oops, sorry about that," Caitlin grinned at him.

For a minute Joey looked dazed. Then he made a big deal of dusting himself off and checking for bruises. "Nothing's broken," he grinned back at her. "For a short girl, you pack some power."

Caitlin laughed and turned back to her locker. She needed her coat, but she wouldn't take mitts. They made her look too young.

"So-o-o, where do you want to go to hit the books?"

Caitlin turned back to Joey. What had he just said?

"Caitlin, don't tell me you forgot?" Joey shook his head. "Partners, right? And I thought Raditch figured you for the smart one of this pair. Man, what I could tell him."

The study sessions. She had completely forgotten. Her hand flew to her mouth. She'd promised Joey they'd study Mondays after school. Automatically her eyes swerved to the front door. She had to go to the Big Seen. She needed to talk to that guy.

Joey's brown eyes were suddenly serious. "We are going to be study partners, aren't we?"

"I can't," Caitlin blurted. "At least, I can't today. Tomorrow, okay? I have to, I have to … go to the dentist. I forgot. I have to go to the dentist. Right now." She looked at her watch. "I have to be there at 4:00. Sorry."

Caitlin slammed her locker shut and ran out the door before even putting on her coat. She was shaking, but not from the cold. Why did Joey always mess things up? She didn't want to lie. He'd looked surprised and sad when she ran out of the school like that.

On the sidewalk, Caitlin stopped to catch her breath and throw on her coat. She could go back in and tell Joey she'd got things mixed up and the study session was back on, after all.

She looked back at the school, then she looked down the street. She turned and started walking.

The Big Seen was empty. Caitlin peered through the display window anxiously. What if he wasn't there? Then she noticed a pair of long legs in tight blue jeans at the level of her nose. He was in the window putting up a poster for a kids' movie, *The Land Before Time*. Her eyes followed the blue jeans up. He was smiling down at her.

"Hi," she said shyly, pushing open the door.

He jumped down from the window, still smiling.

"You showed," he said.

"You said for me to," Caitlin answered.

"Yeah," he acknowledged. "What did you think?"

Caitlin realized he was referring to the movie.

"I just don't want, I mean, it can't ... it mustn't happen," she stammered.

He looked at her, not unkindly. "Got to you, didn't it?" He put his hand on her shoulder and led her towards a chair near the TV set. Then he vaulted onto the counter and sat on it facing her. He seemed a much nicer, friendlier person now.

"It's got a little more to say than *Dirty Dancing*, eh?" he smirked.

"My friends didn't think so," Caitlin said glumly, not daring to look up at him.

"You're not like your friends," he said quietly.

Caitlin's head shot up. How did he know that?

"Most high-school kids don't want to watch anything like that. They don't want to know what people like Caldicott are saying," he continued.

Caitlin nodded. "It is scary what she says."

She was not going to tell him she wasn't in high school, that she was only fourteen. Not right now. "But it made me think. I mean, people who just glance at a nuclear explosion will go blind, even if they are forty miles away." She couldn't stop. "And then she said that even people who made it to fallout shelters would be pressure cooked or asphyxiated because everything within 3,000 square miles would go up in flames. And the fire would eat all the oxygen.

"And then she said that a while ago someone in the States made a mistake and the whole world was on nuclear alert for six minutes.

"I mean, they could have blown us all up. Can you believe that? I mean, I just can't believe it, can you?"

"Yes," he said.

Caitlin was stunned. "You can?"

"Maybe a bomb won't get us, but there are other dangers about life in the nuclear age. Real dangers. Right here."

"Here?" Caitlin squeaked. Then she remembered something."

"You mean Darlington, that big nuclear power plant out on the highway?"

He nodded.

Caitlin remembered visiting the plant with her grade seven class. The guide had been funny, saying nuclear energy wasn't the greatest thing in the world, but that it was pretty cheap and a safe source of electricity. He told them that half of Ontario's energy came from nuclear power, and that when Darlington was operating at full capacity, it would produce enough electricity for just about all of Toronto.

Darlington had been kind of great looking. The nuclear power plant was a sleek grey building that loomed up as you drove to the information centre. The plant was right on the edge of Lake Ontario. It looked like it was coming right out of the water, like some creature from another time.

"So what's the problem with Darlington?" she asked, and then in a rush of courage added, "And what's your name anyway?"

"Robert. And tritium. Ever heard of it?"

Caitlin hadn't.

"It's radioactive. It's a gas and it's one of the leftovers in nuclear reactors. And I'm not the only one who believes it's dangerous. There's a setup at Darlington that removes tritium from what they call heavy water — that's the stuff they store tritium in. They're probably going to sell the tritium."

"What for?" Caitlin was listening carefully.

"Probably to make nuclear bombs," Robert said, turning his steely blue eyes on her. "You know. The kind of bombs you saw in the movie. The kind that leave you glowing in the dark."

"No," Caitlin gasped. "I don't believe it."

"Believe it," he said grimly. "They're going to start hauling trucks loaded with heavy water full of tritium into Darlington. The trucks will come from the nuclear plants up in Bruce County and out in Pickering."

"I don't believe it," Caitlin repeated numbly.

"You will after you read about the first highway accident with one of the trucks. Then we'll have nuclear contaminants seeping into our topsoil, maybe into the water table. Then all the politicians will suddenly care and say they knew all along we shouldn't be trucking tritium. But then it'll be too late."

Caitlin's head was spinning. "But that lady in the movie didn't mention tritium."

Robert threw her a scornful look. "That movie's old. Made in '82."

Caitlin suddenly thought of something. "Why did you let me have it for free?" she asked.

"It's not the store's. It's mine," he replied. He shifted his long lean body on the counter. "Bought it with my first paycheque from here," he said, allowing himself a small proud smile. "A couple of my friends have it, too."

Caitlin was impressed. Imagine having friends like that.

"Have you and your friends talked about it?"

"Yeah. We get together most weeks and update each other on what we've been reading. They're supposed to be issue sessions, but we yell and argue a lot." He flashed that smile again, then stared at her thoughtfully. "Anyone can come," he said slowly. "You can if you want to. It's Tuesdays. Tomorrow. I'll write down the address for you."

"Yes, please. I mean, thanks, I'd love to come." Caitlin couldn't believe this was happening to her.

Robert went behind the counter to find a pencil and sheet of paper.

"Here's how you get to it," he said, sketching a map with a few swift strokes of a felt pen. Caitlin got up and leaned over the counter to look. Their heads were almost touching as they both concentrated on his directions. Neither heard the door of the store open and someone walk in.

"It's a friend of mine's place," Robert was saying. "Get there by eight and I'll make sure I'm there before you."

Caitlin's grateful smile fell from her face. Standing just behind Robert was Joey, glaring at her.

Robert turned around. "Yes?" he said.

Joey scowled at him and took a step or two closer to Caitlin.

"So that's it," he said to her. "The dentist, eh?"

Instinctively Caitlin stepped back, away from Joey and his anger.

"You lied," Joey said, looking straight at her, ignoring Robert, the videos, everything in the store. "Looks like you do a lot of lying."

Caitlin couldn't meet his eyes. She looked around wildly, as if for a hiding place. She felt trapped, frightened.

Her heart was beating wildly. Her face itched as beads of sweat appeared. She didn't want to hear anything more Joey might say.

Robert sensed her panic. "Something you want, buddy?" he said to Joey, coming around to the front of the counter and towering over the boy.

Slowly Joey looked away from Caitlin and up at Robert.

"Not any more," he said in a furious voice.

He turned on his heel and stalked out of the store.

Robert looked back at Caitlin. "Friend of yours?" he asked. Caitlin stared at the door Joey had just banged closed.

"No," she said.

6

It was dark outside. Caitlin pressed her face against the cold glass of the streetcar window as the trolley rattled and jerked along the rutted city street in downtown Toronto.

There were only a few other people on the streetcar with her. Across the aisle, a few rows ahead, was a tired-looking woman loaded down with bags from Honest Ed's bargain emporium. Behind her was a man in a dirty green ski jacket who mumbled to himself and rattled the change in his pockets. Anytime he looked in Caitlin's direction, she whirled her head around and stared out the window. She kept hoping the next stop would be his. But it never was.

At the front of the car near the driver were two boys of about ten, who kept kicking each other with their Reeboks. Caitlin saw the driver watching them in his rearview mirror.

There had been others on board, but they got off at Bathurst Street, where a bus would take them to the subway. Caitlin had barely noticed them go. She was remembering the lie she had told her mother.

Mrs. Ryan had been at the sink peeling potatoes when Caitlin got home from school.

"Thought I'd take the night off," her mother had said cheerfully. "How about hitting the movies with me after dinner? It's been too long, pal."

Of all the nights for her mother to take a break from working. *Just my luck*, she thought. Frantically, Caitlin searched for the right words.

"Sorry, Mom. I can't tonight. I ... I guess I forgot to tell you. I have to go to the library for a ... a study session with this guy in my class."

Caitlin could see a puzzled look cross her mother's face.

"It's something Mr. Raditch is making some of the kids do, to bring up the marks," she hurried on. "Not mine. They're okay. I'm supposed to be helping someone and Tuesday's the only night we could do it."

She smiled apologetically and ran out of the kitchen, her cheeks burning. *Lying* to her mother. Her stomach knotted. In her head she could hear Joey saying, "Looks like you lie a lot." But she knew inside she couldn't tell her the truth, about meeting Robert, about going to this place to learn more about tritium.

Caitlin threw her coat into the closet and ran upstairs to her room. Closing the door, she sat on her bed and thought. There was no other way. She had to lie; she couldn't take the chance her mother might say no. "No" to going downtown by herself at night, and "no" to going to meetings with strange people.

Caitlin stared out the streetcar window and tried to push away all her doubts. She watched the artists selling earrings and belts and tie-dyed T-shirts on the sidewalk, and the cafes crowded with people who all seemed to know each other. And who all dressed in black, Caitlin thought, looking down at her prim camel-hair duffle coat.

All the stores looked fabulous, even from the outside. She couldn't believe the painted wall of the BamBoo restaurant. She strained to catch the sign for Solar Waves. Incredible. A bronzed muscle man in shades, larger than life. She couldn't even spot the names of some of the stores, but then, they didn't really need names. Who could miss the close-up comic-book style drawing of a woman who looked like a Hollywood love goddess of the forties?

It just beats the heck out of malls, she thought.

And the bookstores. There were so many of them, including that one that played the beautiful classical music and was open Sundays. When she was in high school, this is where she wanted to be.

The streetcar shot past The Atomic Rabbit and then Black Head, but Caitlin wasn't watching the street anymore. She was thinking about Joey. That morning she had made up her mind to apologize to him and explain — what? Not about Robert and her going to the meeting, that was for sure. She couldn't tell anyone about that.

No, she was going to explain that it wasn't what it looked like, her and Robert. She'd tell him she really had been on her way to the dentist. Or something. Caitlin sighed. She was not good at lying.

But as it turned out, she didn't have to. Joey had been really friendly. He had made a point of coming up to her at her locker that morning and saying "Hi." Caitlin could not believe her eyes. He'd seemed so friendly.

"Joey, I'm sorry about ...."

"Hey, don't worry. Be happy." Joey had cut off her apologies. "We'll try for next week. Okay?"

Caitlin had been so relieved she'd almost hugged Joey.

"Next week, for sure," she had bubbled.

Joey had leaned against the neighbouring locker, close to her. "Before that, though," he had said in a low intimate voice, "I'll see you at the dance."

Caitlin, suddenly shy and very nervous, had just nodded.

"Okay, then, see you there." Joey had uncurled himself from the locker, pulled at the brim of his hat and sauntered off down the hall.

Caitlin peered back out the streetcar window into the night. Where did Robert's friend live? She looked down at the scrap of paper where she had written 942 Queen

Street West, the address Robert had given her. But the streetcar had shot by all the trendy stores and smart restaurants with their welcoming lights and now was passing darkened, dreary-looking buildings. The sidewalks were empty of people. Her stop was next; Caitlin shivered. What if she just stayed there, safe inside the warm streetcar, to the end of the line, and then rode back to her home and her own bed? But then she'd blow her chance to belong, to be in something that mattered.

She gathered her purse and mitts, slid across the streetcar seat, swayed down the aisle of the car, and got off.

The streetcar rattled away. No one in it gave her a second glance. There was no backing out now. She hoped Robert really was waiting for her. But where was number 942? Robert had said the streetcar stopped right at the door, but she didn't see any door. Right in front of her was a grimy dirt-covered window cracked in one corner. It used to be a store window but now there was a curtain pulled shut across it. All that could be seen was one abandoned pillow, so filthy Caitlin couldn't tell what colour it was.

Caitlin shivered again. This was a horrible place. What was she doing here? She felt something move to one side of her. She screamed, her heart pounded, and her whole body jumped.

A tabby cat lazily detached itself from her leg, pranced over her boots and, with an arrogant flick of the tail, strutted towards a door Caitlin hadn't noticed before. It was set back between the grubby window and a bleak brick building with a hand-scrawled sign saying "Shipping and Receiving Around Back."

It had the numbers 942 painted on it in red.

It doesn't look like a place where anybody would live, Caitlin thought. But she knocked on the door anyway, loudly, persistently. She didn't want to be standing on this deserted dark street any longer.

She heard the sound of boots scrambling down stairs, and first one, then a second deadbolt lock clicking. The door swung open and there stood Robert. The cat leapt past him and straight up the stairs.

For a moment Robert looked off-balance, but when he saw her, he smiled and held the door wide open.

"Hi," he said.

Caitlin followed him up the stairs. There was no hall light and someone had stored a bike in the stairwell. Caitlin stumbled against it; Robert turned and held out his hand. He didn't say a word, nor did he look at her. Caitlin took a deep breath and took his hand. He let it go when she reached the top and gestured to her to follow him down another dingy hallway to the livingroom at the front of the apartment. Her hand still burned where he had held it. But he didn't touch her again or even look at her when he led her into the cluttered, cramped room.

A very tall man standing by the window watched her walk in.

"This is Derek," Robert said. His voice was so low she had to strain to hear him.

Derek was very tall and so thin Caitlin wondered if he had been sick. He was very pale, and his wavy dirty-blond hair was uncombed. He kept running his hands through it. Caitlin noticed that his nails were bitten right down to the quick.

But Derek's deep-brown eyes were so powerful they seem to look through her.

"Hi, we've been waiting for you. Robert told us you were coming this week. Good, we need some new blood." Derek flashed a megawatt smile and Caitlin felt as if a bolt of electricity had shot through her.

It wasn't the same as having a crush on someone. This was something totally different. Caitlin felt charged up, excited, special. What was it they said about people when they described them as "leaders of men"? What was the word they use to describe people who had more than charm, more than power? Charisma, that was it.

And Derek had it.

Robert seemed to dissolve into a corner of the room as Derek introduced her to Karen and Deborah. The two girls were sitting on a dusty, olive-green couch behind Caitlin. Relieved that there were other girls there, Caitlin smiled at them.

But they looked about eighteen. They looked like — Caitlin struggled for the right word — they looked like

Queen Street. Both were dressed totally in black. Deborah, pushing back her long brown hair from her face with a slim, elegant hand, was lighting a cigarette off one held by Karen. She did not look up as she leaned back on the couch and exhaled.

She was beautiful, absolutely beautiful, Caitlin realized with an intake of breath. And glamorous. Along one arm of her black knit tunic, she wore what seemed like dozens and dozens of slim silver bracelets. They shimmered in the room's low light and made a soft, musical sound whenever she moved.

Karen, on the other hand, was not even pretty. Her nose was too long and her face too narrow. But she was dramatic. She had on a floor-length, hooded black robe. Caitlin stared at it. Someone had cut the arms out — otherwise it looked like something a monk might have worn a long, long time ago. Even though it was almost winter, Karen's arms were bare. The better to show off her long, lime-green painted fingernails. She had short hair that had been dyed that strange jet black that was supposed to look phony. Her skin was very white and her eyes looked big and black because she circled them with kohl. She also had on bright red lipstick and wild skeleton earrings that brushed her shoulders.

But then Karen bent down to pick up a book of matches she had dropped and Caitlin's gaze followed her. She could hardly believe her eyes. Karen was wearing Doc

Martens, the thick round-toed boots with coloured laces. Caitlin chewed on her lip. Skinheads wore Doc Martens, and so did a lot of those kids who swarmed other kids in the malls and then stole their leather jackets.

Relax, Caitlin told herself, *these are Robert's friends. Karen wouldn't be a skinhead.*

Karen looked up, but not at Caitlin. Her smile was beamed straight to Derek.

"Hi," Caitlin said anyway, but her voice came out too high. She knew these girls had sized her up during the first thirty seconds she'd been in the room. She also knew had dismissed her as just a kid.

Caitlin felt stupid in her jeans, striped rugby shirt, and blue hightops. She looked so young she might as well have tied a ribbon in her hair, she thought in disgust.

Derek headed back to his spot by the window. There was an old-fashioned oak office chair there and, Caitlin noticed for the first time, a plain plywood table shoved against the window. It was covered in old coffee cups and newspapers and magazines published by environmental groups.

Nobody asked her to sit down. They all had coffee cups but nobody offered her any. She didn't want them to. She didn't drink coffee, and at this point she would die before she'd ask for a glass of milk. Quickly she headed for the empty lopsided, stuffed armchair in the corner and sank gratefully into it. She felt like she wanted to disappear.

Too late she realized that this had been Robert's place. He perched on the arm of it and Caitlin caught the girls exchange a look.

"Robert, there's room here." Deborah uncrossed one long, slim leg and slid down to the end of the sofa. She rested one arm on the sofa arm gracefully and with the other hand patted the now empty spot beside her.

It was mesmerizing. Caitlin had never seen anyone so fluid. She moved like a slow stream of water. As she stared at the beautiful older girl, her heart sank. Deborah was turning the full blast of her beauty onto Robert. Her green, cat-like eyes glittered, her smile beckoned. So this was the "come-hither" look her father sometimes joked that her mother had used to get him to marry her, Caitlin thought. She had better stop thinking about Robert. Nobody stood a chance against Deborah.

But Robert wasn't moving from beside her. Next to her, Caitlin sensed his body stiffen, then relax.

"I'm okay here," he said curtly.

A silence fell on the room as three pairs of eyes stared at Caitlin. *What have I got myself into?* she thought to herself as she listened to her heart pound frantically.

7

"We usually start our sessions talking about what's been in the papers lately," Derek quickly explained to Caitlin, filling the awkward silence. "But there's been damn little all week, and maybe we should talk about that."

Caitlin hated people swearing. Her eyes darted around the room. It was dingy and dirty, and who were these people anyway? She shouldn't have come.

"People are so wrapped up in their stupid blue boxes they think the problem's solved," Robert grumbled.

Karen laughed. "Yeah, they think they've saved the world with a plastic box."

Caitlin pulled her coat tighter around her, burrowing inside it. She didn't like what they were saying. She favoured the city's recycling program — and the bright blue boxes they gave everyone for their glass and cans. But she couldn't say it. She was too scared. Deborah was the only one who even bothered to look at her, but they were scornful looks. Caitlin wished she were somewhere else.

"Well, the world will go away if they put boxes over their heads," Robert muttered. They all laughed, especially Deborah.

Caitlin squirmed. Robert was grinning in the direction of the couch. Maybe he and Deborah were together, after all. Maybe Robert just wanted to sit in his chair, maybe that's why he's sitting so close to her. Maybe she should try and think of a way she could leave — soon.

Instead Caitlin heard herself say, "I don't get it."

Derek whirled to face her. "It's like Nero fiddling while Rome burned. We're going to fry, too — someday and somehow — if we don't get beyond the small stuff and look at the big picture."

His long legs covered the room in three strides. Suddenly he was looming right before her. Kneeling down, he looked intently into her eyes.

"Look," he said, as if they were the only people in the room. "Of course we're in favour of anything that helps the environment. We're not crazy people. Of course we know the recycling program is wonderful. We're glad people finally care about the chemical content of the water they drink. We're especially glad smart people aren't polluting the air with their cigarette smoke anymore." He turned towards the couch. Deborah seemed unconcerned, but she butted out her cigarette; Karen looked guilty. "And we're glad people are now worried about losing the ozone layer, the only thing between us and the sun's ultraviolet rays."

"That's not small stuff," Caitlin replied, looking at her lap. Derek rocked back on his heels and looked at her with a new expression on his face. Was it respect?

"The point is," Karen was looking at Derek eagerly, wanting him to approve, "people have forgotten about the really big problem of atomic bombs. Everybody loves Gorbachev now that he's the leader of the Soviet Union. They all believe him when he says Russia will back down even more on their missile production, and now everybody thinks the nuclear problem is over."

Caitlin wished know-it-all Kathleen could hear this.

"Caldicott's not pulling in the crowds," Derek said.

"Practically nobody ever asks for the video anymore," Robert chimed in. "Caitlin's the only one the whole time I've been at the store. Most people have never heard of the movie."

"But I had never heard of the movie until you showed it in the store. How was I supposed to know about it?" Caitlin protested.

"Where have you been?" Deborah frowned. "It won an Oscar in 1983 and then the United States government decided it was propaganda and said they didn't approve of it. Everybody knew about that."

Caitlin stared at the wall behind Deborah. Where had she been in 1983? Playing with her dolls, that's where. She was experiencing something like a sinking feeling. She was in over her head.

"Yeah, everybody knew about it. That year. Then everybody let it slide away. They forgot. It's easier not to think too much about this kind of stuff." Robert sounded bitter. "You know, once upon a time there used to be demonstrations, marches — big ones with thousands of people — to change things."

He gave a short laugh. "They even had sit-ins. Believe it. People would storm offices — they used to do it at universities a lot back in the sixties — and they would not leave until they got what they wanted."

He fell silent. No one in the room spoke.

Caitlin was afraid to even breathe. Robert sprang from the seat and stood facing the small group with his hands on his hips. He glared at them.

"Nobody's going to the wall for what they believe these days. Nobody. We're not. The kids in school aren't. Nobody gives a ..."

"Robert, for crying out loud. We were just talking about the women of Greenham Common last week. You can't say they haven't done something." Karen sounded exasperated.

Caitlin frowned. The women of what? She'd never heard of them. "Who?" she blurted.

She saw Deborah roll her eyes at Karen. Caitlin thought, *what's with this girl, anyway?* She didn't know Caitlin at all, but she seemed to hate her. And all Caitlin had done so far was ask a couple of questions.

Suddenly it dawned on her. Robert had asked her to come here, and he was sitting beside her on the chair. Deborah didn't like her because she was jealous. Was Deborah Robert's girlfriend, then? That thought worried Caitlin. Robert didn't seem to be paying much attention to Deborah's mood. He was looking at Derek, who nodded.

"They are really amazing." Robert began. "Last week, we did a lot of reading and found out a lot about these women. This was one of the most effective peace protests in the world. Since 1981, some of them have been camped out at Greenham Common, no matter what the weather. Once there were thousands, now there probably aren't a hundred, maybe not even twenty, but it is a real peace community."

He twisted around so he could look right at Caitlin. "And they're not giving up, even though the Russians and Americans say they'll have all the missiles out of there soon. The women are monitoring to make sure the missiles are removed safely. And they are still protesting because none of the warheads are being destroyed, but just shipped back to Europe."

"Back up a little and explain to her that these women have been camped around this British Air Force base about fifty miles outside London, England," Derek interrupted.

Caitlin wondered if he was a teacher. He seemed to like explaining and organizing.

"They were upset with the military base being there," he continued, seeing Caitlin's puzzled frown, "because it was also a resting ground for a lot of American nuclear missiles. This was supposed to be one of those pretty rural areas of England, but somehow it was the site the Western world powers chose for its nuclear war strategy back then."

Cheerfully interrupting each other, Derek and Robert built a rich picture of how these women had lived. Caitlin could almost see the few ragtag tents, the mud, the seven forbidding gates protecting the army base.

The women cooked and got their heat from campfires; they slept all bundled up in pup tents. They didn't have much in the way of pots or pans, because the local police usually confiscated what they could when they paid their daily visit. It was against a local bylaw to camp on public property, but the Greenham women fought that rule too.

Once a day they tapped a fire hydrant — their only way to get water. There was no electricity. Even portable toilets were a luxury because the police also took them away to try to get the women to leave.

Some women had left their families to join the vigil; some had brought their children to the site to live with them in the mud and the mess. Some students had left school to stay for a while; some of the women were grand-mothers. Some were from homes close by; others came from countries like the United States. They were all afraid of nuclear war.

Derek got up and walked over to his desk. He picked up a few newspapers and magazines.

"Most of these are a couple of years old," he said. "Not much has been written about the women lately. Just short articles about how some of them are still there, watching them dismantle. I guess they're not news now. But some of the writers used to make the women out to be real warriors, real heroes."

Caitlin glanced through the material. Derek was right. Her eye caught adjectives like "courageous" and descriptions that began with the words "warrior queens." She closed her eyes. Imagine giving up your life and everyone you loved to go and fight for a cause. Well, not giving up a life exactly, since there was no mention of any of the women dying, but they sure had given up their comfortable middle-class homes.

These women know how to get right to what really counts, Caitlin thought. They must have been an inspiration to all the people in the world, but especially to the people living near the nuclear missile base.

"Are the other people who live there really supporting them and helping them out?" Caitlin asked.

She was surprised when Karen answered her. For the first time, the girl with the dark eyes spoke to Caitlin.

"You've hit on it with that question," she said. "I thought that, too. Sisterhood, eh? We read some stuff last week that said some people helped out the women with food and clothes, but a lot of the locals started to hate them. They thought they were dirty; they thought they were troublemakers; they thought they were all gay because they wouldn't let men in the protest — since, of course, it is men who run the army. Here, read this." Karen got up from the couch, took the pile of newspapers and magazines from Caitlin's lap, and leafed through it until she found an article to hand to Caitlin.

Bending over Caitlin, she pointed to a spot in an old newspaper story. The reporter had noticed a sign in the window of a tearoom in the nearest town that read: "No Greenham Women Allowed."

Caitlin was appalled. "That's disgusting. How could people be so cruel?"

Robert smiled grimly. "I don't know how, but they can be."

Derek was back at his command post by the window. He swivelled the wooden chair to get his long legs up on one of the piles of papers on the table. Then he asked, "But what, in the end, are these mighty women accomplishing? What, in a word, is the point?"

Caitlin was speechless. How dare he ask that? She crossed her arms defiantly over her chest. She was no longer under Derek's spell.

But on the arm of Caitlin's chair, Robert sat forward. Caitlin could sense his excitement. And both Karen and Deborah sat quietly and attentively.

"They did it because they had to, and that's all that matters," Karen said.

"No way. They did it because it was the only way to get people to pay attention to the problem," Robert shouted.

"Maybe," Derek sounded sly, "they did it because they were bored with the lives they had in their neat little houses."

"And maybe they didn't," Karen cried back.

Caitlin followed the debate the way she would watch one of her father's tennis matches — eyes on the conversation ball as it bounced back and forth from player to player. But this was more exciting than any tennis game. She'd never heard an argument like this before.

Here she was in a room with four others — maybe university students — who were really talking about the issues that mattered.

They were not talking about clothes or boys or records, but about nuclear war and fighting back and changing things. And she, Caitlin Ryan, was right here with them.

Deborah had also just been listening. Looking at her watch, she stood and announced it was 9:30 p.m. and that everyone wanting to hear Taborah Johnson's set at the Cameron House should leave now.

Derek and Karen went to get their coats. Caitlin shyly looked at Robert. Was he going, too? But he got up from the arm of the chair, held out a hand to help her up, and asked if she was taking the eastbound streetcar home.

Caitlin nodded.

"I'll go with you, then," he said.

She could feel Deborah's eyes boring a hole into her back.

"Robert," the girl called. "Catching the set?"

"Nope." He showed no reaction to the flash of anger in her eyes. Without another word, Deborah stalked out of the apartment. Derek and Karen hurried to catch up with her.

"Lock up, will you?" Derek called out to Robert.

Robert nodded and waited for Caitlin at the door. Checking to make sure it was locked, he gestured for her to follow him down the dark stairwell. Outside they waited for a streetcar to come. This time Caitlin felt safe and protected in the dark, dismal street. Robert was a head taller than she was. His leather bomber jacket smelled of pipe tobacco — probably somebody else's, because he didn't smoke. It was old and worn and comforting.

"Want to come back next week?" he asked suddenly.

Caitlin's eyes widened. Would she? Try keeping her away. The streetcar rattled up to their stop. There was time to collect her thoughts as they climbed on board and found a seat together near the back.

"I really enjoyed it. I learned so much. I really want to come back. I'd like to come next week," she said. It was easier to talk to him while she was looking straight ahead.

"You like us, then?" he asked.

If only you knew, Caitlin thought to herself, but said only, "Sure."

Robert told her he had not been too sure about how she would react to his friends.

"Karen and Deborah aren't always … friendly," he shrugged. "Karen would want to make sure Derek doesn't pay too much attention to you."

And Deborah, thought Caitlin, *won't like it if you pay too much attention to me.* She wondered whether they were a couple like Karen and Derek. They couldn't be, she told herself, or else he wouldn't be sitting here on the streetcar with me.

But Deborah was so beautiful. Her clothes, her long hair, all those bracelets …

Caitlin gazed at her duffle coat and sighed. She couldn't compete with someone like that.

She couldn't compete with anyone, she was too shy anyway.

"I, I'm not really into that," she stammered, realizing Robert was waiting for her reply. "I just liked being with intelligent people who talk about important things."

Robert nodded. "I thought you would like it."

The questions that had been building inside her all night burst forth. Where did they get all their information? There were loads of pamphlets and letters and books on Derek's desk. Was he a researcher? How did the four of them get together? Were there other people, like herself, who dropped in some weeks? Did they have a name?

No name, Robert told her, and sure there were others

who dropped in from time to time, but those four were the group. Robert and Derek had gone to high school together.

"Derek's at the university — first year. Taking philosophy and political science." Robert said. "He works some afternoons in the library. That's how he's got all those articles."

"Why does he live in that apartment?"

There was a long pause. Caitlin began to think maybe she shouldn't have asked.

Then Robert told her Derek had moved out of his parents' house halfway through last year when he was in grade thirteen. He was fed up with their values; they were fighting a lot, too. To get through the year he worked as a bicycle courier, which explained the bike Caitlin had fallen over in the hallway.

"He pulled it off, too," Robert said admiringly. "Derek's smart and he's happier living alone. He got his year and he got high enough marks to get into university."

But he added that he thought Derek was trying to do too much with school work and his jobs and that was why he, Robert, had decided to take a year off and work before going to university.

"But I didn't think working in the Big Seen would be so mindless," he said. "After you've seen one movie, you've seen them all. They're all about nothing important and everything dumb."

He's so intelligent, Caitlin thought. *And so easy to talk to. He talks about important things.* She felt she could ask him anything. They rode along in silence for a minute or two. But even that felt comfortable now.

"Tell me about the girls," she asked him.

Deborah, he said, was studying to be a jewellery designer. He didn't know her very well; she was Karen's friend, really. And Karen, well, she was in some of Derek's classes at university.

Caitlin was dying to know more about Deborah; she wanted to know more about what he felt about Deborah. But by now she had realized that Robert, basically, was a quiet person.

When he said something, it meant something.

She felt him shift in the seat beside her, moving a little away from her. Quickly she looked over at him. Robert was getting up. They were at Yonge Street.

"My stop," he said. He paused for a moment then said. "I'm going for a beer. Want to come along?"

Caitlin sat up with a jolt. A beer? How old did he think she was? "No. I mean no, thanks," she said. "I've got to get home." She smiled at him.

"Come round to the store Monday. It's our slow day," he said.

Monday. Joey. Robert was staring at her with his serious blue gaze, waiting for her answer.

"Sure," Caitlin said.

8

One hour and ten minutes before Degrassi's first bell went off, Caitlin walked through the school's big double doors.

The halls were empty. The click of her boots on the marble floor echoed off the walls as she walked purposefully to the *Digest* office.

"Hey, grab a stapler. Well, no, not yet, but grab a pen," Trish called out cheerfully as Caitlin opened the office door. The table was covered with pages, twelve in all, and articles were stacked beside each page. The November *Digest*.

Caitlin smiled, threw her coat on a nearby chair, and leaned over the table to check the front page for any spelling or typographical mistakes. That chore first, then laying out the stories on the inside pages, then writing all the headlines.

But something caught her eye. She made a clucking sound. It was the front page, just as Mr. Raditch had ordered — a huge drawing of the Degrassi sweatshirt he wanted everybody to come to the dance to order. Caitlin looked at it closely. Not bad.

"Who'd he get to draw this?" she asked Trish.

"Diana. Good, isn't it?"

Caitlin nodded, still staring at the layout the teacher had worked out. Mr. Raditch had listened to her after all. It wasn't all art. There, in a column down one side of the front page, was her story about the dance and Murray Cram. Not the kind of story she really wanted carrying her name on the front page, but at least he had agreed with her that there should be some words there.

She picked up a pencil and chewed on it, trying to think up a headline. "Dressing for a cause"? "Good time gear"? Yeah, that one. It fit the space, too. Caitlin wrote it out, measuring the size of letters needed.

"Good stuff." Trish was looking over her shoulder. "You're getting pretty fast at this."

"Practice," Caitlin laughed, writing the caption to go underneath Diana's drawing.

Eagerly she reached for page two. She loved this part, when she could see all the bits and small pieces of the *Digest* finally come together to become a newspaper, something people could hold in their hands, read, and talk about.

"Let's move the basketball story to the top of the page, put the league standings in a separate story, and have the team's picture bigger, but on the bottom," she said to Trish, reaching for the scissors.

Trish grabbed the gluepot and a fresh piece of paper, and swiftly put together the new layout.

"You're right. That looks better," she said, throwing the page back at Caitlin. "Headline, madame?"

"Degrassi on a winning streak," Caitlin immediately replied.

Trish stood shaking her head. "Caitlin, you are hot. We're going to have this done before class starts. Keep this up and we won't have to do anything but staple after school."

Caitlin smiled at her friend. She was surprised at how easily everything was coming to her this morning. She must be operating on the energy left over from Robert and his friends last night.

She had got home before 10:00 so her mother wasn't worried or suspicious. Her Dad had just laughed at her for turning into a study-aholic, as he called her.

It took a long time to get to sleep. She had been thinking about those brave women in England, about Karen's green nails. And about Robert too. He really was nice. Nice to talk to. Nice clothes, too. That jacket looked so smooth, she had wanted to touch it. It didn't look like the leather gear the kids at Degrassi wore; it looked old, not new from a store. Maybe it belonged to someone else. Maybe his father, maybe he had worn it in the war.

Caitlin reached for the third and fourth pages of the *Digest*. Better think about editing Kathleen's story on school uniforms. She wasn't angry about running it anymore. She didn't need to fight it as much now that she had Robert and his friends to talk to about the really important things.

So the stories seemed to arrange themselves this morning. The headlines — exactly the right ones — seem to pop out of her effortlessly. "Go with the flow," she said out loud, presenting two more finished pages to Trish with a flourish.

"Absolutely," said Trish, reaching for them.

They worked quickly and efficiently together for another twenty-five minutes until they heard the sounds of the rest of the students in the school corridor outside their door.

"Time's up," said Trish. "Mr. Raditch won't believe this. We've done all the pages. You can give them to him now and he can get them run off this morning. We can start stapling at lunch and finish up right after school. Incredible."

"It's just as well, Trish," Caitlin laughed. "We've got to sell the *Digest* tomorrow, otherwise forget it. The dance is this Friday, yikes."

This Friday. Caitlin kept the smile on her face as she carried the finished pages out of the office and laid them on her teacher's desk in the classroom. The dance! Should she go? Would anyone dance with her? Would Joey? He'd seemed all right yesterday, but Caitlin wondered.

She sat down at her desk and opened her books. Maybe she just wouldn't go. She'd visit the library and try to find some magazine or newspaper stories on those women in England, that's what she'd do.

"Caitlin," Melanie was whispering to her from the next desk. "Can you come to my place tonight after school?"

"Can't," Caitlin whispered back. "Got to work on the *Digest.*"

Melanie's face fell. "Tomorrow night then, okay?"

Caitlin nodded.

"I need you to help me figure out what to wear Friday. And Mom says you can come to my house for pizza before we go to the dance, okay?"

Caitlin looked at Melanie. She was becoming a friend. It would be good to have a close friend at Degrassi again.

"Okay," she said.

Heaps of clothes were piled all over Melanie's bed.

"It's no use. I'll never look like you," she wailed.

Caitlin burst out laughing. "Count yourself lucky. Better to look like you than me."

"Don't pretend to be ugly now," Melanie moaned.

"Who's pretending?"

Caitlin was sitting at Melanie's desk leafing through her friend's copy of the school paper. It had sold out yesterday. People were excited about the new Degrassi sweats and about Murray Cram coming to the school. She put down the paper and sighed. The dance started in one hour. She was dreading it.

She glanced at Melanie's full-length mirror and frowned. Maybe she should have worn a whole bunch of bracelets, like Deborah. Or done something wild like paint her nails green like Karen.

But all she had done was put on a wide silver belt over the same black knit dress she wore everywhere and pile her hair up at the back. Did it make her look a little older?

"I still look fourteen," she groaned out loud.

"Well, you are fourteen," answered Melanie. "You want to look like Joey's mother? Help me decide which one to wear."

She held up two hangers. On one was a wild neon orange overblouse Caitlin had never seen before, on the other hung a huge men's striped cotton shirt, the kind of thing Melanie wore to school a lot.

"Where did you get that one?" Caitlin pointed to the orange shirt, shading her eyes.

"It's my mom's," said Melanie. "Do you think it's too much?"

"No, wear it. It's great," Caitlin said.

She loved it. Besides, if Melanie wore it, no one would notice dowdy Caitlin next to her in her boring black dress.

Melanie's mother dropped them off at the school right at 7:30 p.m.

"My mom's always on time," Melanie explained to Caitlin as they ran straight to the washroom. "I tried to tell her you don't go to dances early, but she wouldn't listen.

Did you notice if the guys are here yet?"

Caitlin hadn't, but then she hadn't looked round at anyone. Her hands felt sweaty and she was sure everyone could hear her heart pounding. This was only the second dance she had ever been to. Last year's graduating dance had been the first.

Joey had been the only boy who had asked her to dance. Caitlin squirmed as she remembered. She had stepped on his feet because she was so nervous. She wasn't a very good dancer anyway.

"Come on, let's get out of here and find the guys," Melanie said to her, pulling her out of the washroom. "Snake said they'd be here about now."

Music was already coming from the gym. The Rolling Stones' Steel Wheels. It sounded great. Murray Cram must have brought his own sound system. In spite of herself, Caitlin wondered what the popular deejay looked like. She followed Melanie into the gym, staring at the side of the stage where a middle-aged man in a crewneck sweater was playing records.

"He looks like my father, only fatter," Caitlin said. She tugged on Melanie's shirt to get her attention. "Look at Murray Cram," she hissed.

Melanie didn't hear her. She was scanning the crowd for a sign of Snake. She didn't see him come through the door behind her and stand beside her.

"Hi," he said, and his smile included Caitlin.

"Hi," Caitlin and Melanie replied. Then Melanie asked, "Where's Joey?"

Snake looked uncomfortable. "He's coming now," he said, shifting from one leg to another. "Want to dance?"

"Hey, my man," Joey hollered out.

Melanie took Snake's hand and smiled at Caitlin.

"Hey," Joey repeated as he walked by the trio. With one hand he tipped his hat to them. His other arm was around Liz's shoulders.

"Are we ready to boogie?" he yelled. "C'mon, what are we waiting for."

Melanie threw Caitlin a look of sympathy as Snake pulled her onto the floor.

Liz coolly glanced over at Caitlin. "Nice belt," she said.

The grade nine girl with the punk haircut and sardonic mouth had always intimidated Caitlin, but she managed to stammer her thanks.

Joey pretended he had just noticed Caitlin standing there.

"Oh, Caitlin," he said, still holding Liz. "Hi."

"Hi," Caitlin answered, looking straight into his brown eyes. They were sparkling; they were triumphant. He was paying her back for finding her with Robert.

Caitlin felt her nails digging into the palms of her hands. She made herself unclench them. She would not care. She did not care.

"Have fun," she said. And turned and walked through

the crowd out of the gym, and out of the school.

Now she was thankful Melanie's mother had delivered them to the dance so early. There was still time to go to the library.

9

"I got the greatest idea at the library this weekend."

Caitlin's voice was brimming with excitement as she told Trish her plan for the December *Degrassi Digest*. A recycling campaign, starting with the newspaper itself. Print it on recycled paper. Get bins to put around the school for the all the paper the school uses. Get a recycling company to come and pick up the paper.

"I've even got the headline. Want to hear it?" she asked Trish.

"Love to," answered a deep baritone voice.

Mr. Raditch walked into the Digest office, glancing at his watch. "It's 8:15 a.m. on Monday. Isn't it a little early for plotting?"

Caitlin grinned at the teacher. He knew they were meeting this morning to get an early start on the next issue. Last week he had told Caitlin that this month's *Digest* was the best ever, and he had said, with a wink, that the paper was just about ready for one of her issue pieces.

"So what is the headline for this yet-to-be-written award-winning story by Caitlin Ryan, editor extraordinaire?" he said, settling into one of the straight-back chairs around the table and carefully placing a large parcel on the floor near him.

"Recycle Christmas," Caitlin said. There was a silence. She looked over at Trish's startled face and at Mr. Raditch's stern one. "Oh, all right. How about The Gift of Recycling?

Mr. Raditch's face relaxed. "Better, much better."

Caitlin ran through the idea again. It had been forming in her mind all weekend. After the dance — she shook away the thought — at the library she had found some fascinating newspaper articles about the women of Greenham Common. There must be something they could do at Degrassi. Recycling was a start, even though it was a small one.

Mr. Raditch was listening to her ideas attentively.

"It could work," he said, slowly. "But it would take a lot of work to start it up. You won't get it organized in time for our December issue, I'm afraid. January might be better."

Caitlin felt her shoulders relax. A delay of one month she could handle. At least he hadn't said no.

"There's another reason you won't have enough time to organize a recycling program this month," Mr. Raditch continued. "I want to tell you about it. Look."

He bent down and hauled the parcel from the floor

onto the table. Opening it, he laid out half a dozen of the *Degrassi Digest* sweatshirts on the table.

"Ohhh, they're here," Trish gasped.

"Just a few are here. And they're yours," the teacher replied, handing one to each girl. "The kids who ordered theirs at the dance will have to wait a little longer for theirs."

"Thanks," Caitlin said. "How much do I owe you for mine?"

Mr. Raditch grinned. "Nothing. You'll be working for them. Just listen."

He explained that next Monday would be *Degrassi Digest* Day. There would be a special assembly which would feature a speech on Degrassi and its newspaper and how, as Mr. Raditch put it, one can't exist without the other.

"I want all the staff on stage wearing a sweatshirt," he said, wagging a forefinger. "But I want this to be the first time anyone else in the school sees them, understand?"

Caitlin and Trish nodded.

The bell sounding the start of school went off. Mr. Raditch leaped from his seat, stuffed the sweatshirts back in the bag and put the bag in a corner of the office.

At the door he paused for a moment.

"By the way," he said. "That speech on Degrassi and the *Digest* and how they need each other? I want you to give it, Caitlin."

He closed the door, leaving Trish and Caitlin both speechless.

"Wow," Trish finally said, getting up and heading for the door. "Good luck, Caitlin."

For a few seconds Caitlin sat by herself in the deserted office. A speech in front of the entire school? Just the thought of it gave her the shakes.

She got up and headed to her classroom, lost in thought. Finally, she would have a chance to talk about what a newspaper really could do, what a school newspaper could encourage its readers to think about and possibly act on. Caitlin walked a little faster. This was a wonderful break. So what if making speeches made her nervous? This was worth a little suffering. She gave Melanie a huge smile as she met the girl outside the classroom door.

"Hey, how'd it go Friday?" She wanted Melanie to know she didn't care, that she was all right.

Melanie didn't meet her eye. "All right, I guess," she gulped, ducking her head and sinking into her own seat.

"Great," Caitlin replied, but she felt a twinge inside. Melanie was still really embarrassed for her. She wanted to tell Melanie she didn't care, but she didn't know how.

Caitlin frowned. If she told Melanie why Joey had snubbed her, that Joey was paying her back because she stood him up to meet Robert, there was a chance Melanie might tell the other kids. Caitlin didn't know why, but she knew deep down that she didn't want anybody at Degrassi hearing about Robert and Derek and the group.

Caitlin slowly unpacked her notebooks and thoughtfully lined up her pens on the desk. She really liked Melanie. She wanted to be friends. Good friends. Just this weekend she had missed her and wanted to phone her and ask her about the dance.

As for Joey, there was no way to repair that mess-up. Unless she stopped seeing Robert on Mondays and begged — Caitlin smirked to herself — Joey for another chance to be study partners.

No. She wanted those times with Robert. Today she wanted to ask him what she should say in her speech about the role of the press. He'd know.

"What do I think of papers?" Robert looked up from the newspaper he was reading and gave Caitlin one of his rare smiles. "When I read this stuff, not much." Caitlin leaned over to look at what he was reading. "Darlington to Fire Up Fourth Reactor," the headline said.

"The more nuclear power we generate, the more we depend on it. And the greater the chance of an accident like the one at Three Mile Island in the States," Robert said, all traces of the smile gone.

"That's not good." She turned to glance at him. She gave a slight start. He had bent over to look at the article as well and his face was just an inch from hers. He was so close she could touch his cheek if she moved even the smallest fraction. But she couldn't move; it was like she was under a spell.

He broke it when he got up and stared out the store window.

"It's not great news," he said sadly. "We're losing it."

"Losing what?" Caitlin wanted to know.

"The fight, the war," he said ruefully. "There's just not enough of us worried about the danger of becoming more and more dependent on nuclear power."

Caitlin wanted to console him. "Maybe other people will read the paper and get scared and worried just like you did. That's what a newspaper is for — to alert people. So maybe they can stop it. It doesn't mean it has to happen."

Robert gazed at her for a moment.

"You into journalism?" he asked.

Caitlin felt herself blush. Eagerly she told him about the *Digest* and about the special assembly. And about her speech.

Robert listened thoughtfully. "So you're the editor of your school paper?" he said. "Is this what you want to get into later?"

Caitlin nodded. "I think so. Yes."

"Because you want to cover issues, not rock concerts, right?"

Robert was testing her.

"No rock concerts, absolutely not."

"You a good writer?" he asked.

Caitlin hesitated. "Not bad," she said truthfully.

Robert folded up the paper. He was quiet, obviously

thinking something over. "You're coming to Derek's tomorrow, aren't you?" he said. "You did say you would."

His blue eyes seemed to be drilling right into her.

"Of course," Caitlin said weakly.

The door opened. Two eleven-year-old boys pushed each other into the store, coming to a standstill in front of the life-size Indiana Jones floor display.

Robert and Caitlin looked at each other. Robert made a face and got up to help the boys.

Caitlin knew it was time for her to go. Reluctantly she walked to the door.

"So it's tomorrow for sure, then?" Robert called after her. She turned and nodded.

He stood there, tall and straight and serious. His eyes locked into hers.

"The thing is," he said, "we really need someone who writes."

10

Derek's front door was ajar. They must be expecting me, Caitlin thought, eagerly climbing the dark stairwell.

"You got here." Robert unfolded his long legs and crossed the room to meet her.

Derek and Karen were turned away from the door, bent over the cluttered table studying an open newspaper. Karen turned around and gave Caitlin a friendly wave.

"Robert says you're a writer," she called. "Do we ever need you now."

Caitlin stole a glance at the battered green couch. It was empty. Where was Deborah this week?

Derek seemed distracted; he began to pace the room.

"What's the matter?" Caitlin asked Robert in a low voice.

"They're starting up one of the nuclear reactors at Darlington." Karen answered, pointing to the newspaper.

It was the one Robert had been reading yesterday in the Big Seen. Caitlin's mind raced back to one of the first times she and Robert had talked. What else had he said then about the dangers of Darlington? Something about transporting some substance used to make nuclear weapons in heavy water, whatever that meant.

Robert rifled through a pile of newspaper clippings on Derek's table and pulled out one. "Look at this article," he said, waving a piece of paper in his hand. Caitlin could just make out the headline: "The failure of Canada's anti-nuclear crusaders."

"This writer calls us duds."

"Which we are," Karen said ruefully.

"What do you need a writer for?" Caitlin interrupted.

Derek stopped pacing and stood in front of her. Bending down so his eyes met hers, his hands gripped both her forearms urgently.

"We have to get a press release out. Tonight," he said. "Can you do it for us?"

A press release, a statement that went out to all the media, newspapers, and radio and television stations. She had never written one before. Derek's eyes demanded an answer; meekly she agreed to do it.

"I'll write it, but I don't know how to set it up. I don't know what a press release should look like," she confessed.

"No problem. We do." Karen stabbed at the newspaper article with her long nails. This week they were painted red. Against the paper, they resembled bright drops of blood.

"Look, we've got all the information we could ever need here. Here's something about a government study they're doing in the States on the number of cancer deaths of people who live near nuclear power plants. They've noticed a lot of people getting leukemia.

"Here's another article. Look at that headline: 'Could Chernobyl Happen Here? YES. Striking Similarities Between CANDU and Soviet Design ... Troubling for Canadians.'"

Karen put down the paper. "So the nuclear reactor that Darlington just fired up is a CANDU. And the CANDU, this guy says, is a lot like the reactor the Russians have. The one that caused the nuclear catastrophe in Chernobyl in 1986 that covered parts of Russia and Finland with radiation."

Derek interrupted her.

"The people in the town — and some people on the Atomic Energy Control Board — were never that happy with the Darlington computer system that shuts down the reactor system in an emergency. The Board stalled for about a year because they didn't think the emergency system was safe."

"So is it safe now?" Caitlin asked. She sat in the nearest chair and fished for a pen and paper in her bag. She had better take notes. This was not going to be easy. They wanted the press release to state everything they knew about the dangers of nuclear power.

"Maybe we should ask the Russians. Is nuclear power in the middle of three million people ever safe?" Robert sounded impatient. "And do any of these three million people care? What is anybody out there doing about this?"

If only he knew, Caitlin thought, what she had done to be there with them. She had lied to her mother again, told her she was studying with Joey. Her mother had hugged her and said she was proud Caitlin was using her time to help another student.

"People care, but maybe they're afraid to know. I think I was before I met you guys," Caitlin said.

The others stared at her.

"I think she's right," said Derek. "Nobody wants any more nuclear plants in Canada. Remember that report the government got a year or two ago stating that?"

"Yeah, I remember it," Robert said sadly. "Big deal. It was a little late to come out with that recommendation when Canada already had nineteen reactors and 12,000 tonnes of radioactive waste from them that no one knows what to do with."

"No use expecting action from politicians," said Karen vehemently.

"So I guess it's up to us," Caitlin said, looking round the room at the others, "to show that people are worried and do care."

The room fell silent. Karen looked at Derek, who turned to Robert. Finally Derek said, "But how?"

"Why don't we get some people and some tents and do something like the women of Greenham Common? I've been thinking about them ever since you told me about them," Caitlin suggested.

Shyly she looked at the others. She could just imagine what they were thinking. Why couldn't she keep a lid on things, think before she opened her mouth? She stared down at the floor. She'd made sure she had worn black, not that stupid striped rugby jersey she had worn last time, because she didn't want to look like a kid. It didn't matter now. She had opened her mouth and now they really were going to think she was dumb.

But Karen was looking at Derek, who was staring at his hands on his lap.

Suddenly he reached over and took the pen from Karen's hand. "Forget the press release," he said. "We've been talking too long. It's time to do something."

Karen threw back her head and laughed.

"Hallelujah," she crowed, throwing both arms in the air. "Let's go for it."

Derek smiled at Karen. "Getting itchy feet?"

"We've been sitting here week after week. All we do is talk. You bet."

"Yeah, it's time," Derek agreed.

But Karen wasn't finished. She pointed to Caitlin, "And it took our newest member to show us how."

Caitlin sank into the hard back of her chair.

Member. Karen had called her a member. She was in, one of them. And they liked the idea. They were going to do it. *No, we're going to do it*, Caitlin corrected herself. *I'm in this, too.*

"Not so fast." Robert threw Caitlin a look that chilled her before he turned his full attention on Derek. "Let's think about this first. We need to talk —"

Karen groaned. "We don't need to talk. We've talked, talked, talked too damn much." She struck a cheerleader-type pose. "Action. Action. We want action."

Derek and Caitlin both laughed at Karen in her Doc Martens and weird unnatural black hair imitating a fresh-faced high-school cheerleader. Even Robert smiled. A little.

Derek pulled the oak chair closer to the table. He grabbed Caitlin's notepad and pen.

"Okay, now. What we want is some sort of tent city. Right on the Darlington site. And soon. Say, December 1?" He looked at Karen and Caitlin, who nodded. Robert stalked across the room, away from the group bending over the desk.

"There won't be any water or any of the conveniences there, so we'll have to provide everything we need our-selves. How many tents can we get? Have you got one at home?" he asked Karen.

"We've got a couple of old ones at home," she replied. "My parents used to drag my sister and me out camping when we were kids."

Caitlin tried to imagine Karen as a kid in a campground. It was hard.

"How about you, Caitlin?" Derek was looking at her.

Caitlin jumped. Out of the corner of her eye she had been watching Robert. Why wasn't he saying anything? Why was he sitting by himself on the musty couch?

She gulped. "My father has a tent."

"Tents!" Robert broke into the discussion. His blue eyes were glinting with anger. "Tents. What do tents have to do with stopping nuclear reactors? This is nuts. It's a stupid idea and it's illegal. You'll get arrested."

Derek carefully put down his pen. He slowly unfolded his tall frame from the chair and stood up. Looking down at Robert, he said in a cold voice, "So?"

The two friends faced each other, neither dropping their gaze.

Karen touched Caitlin's arm.

"I think we'll be off now," she said hurriedly, pulling Caitlin up and away from the table. "See you."

Caitlin scooped up her coat as she was pulled past the couch. "I'll see you next week, okay?" was all she had time to say before Karen had pushed them both out of the door.

"Whew," the older girl said as they reached the street. She lit a cigarette, exhaling slowly. "I've been dying for one of these. Want one?" She shoved the pack at Caitlin, who shook her head.

Karen took another drag. "It was a good time to leave.

The guys have to work out a few things. No sweat. The Darlington Demo is off and running."

She exhaled and frowned. "But we need to pull together some fact sheets. Information packages to hand out to reporters." She grinned. "And to the crowds who'll gather round to worship us."

Caitlin's head was spinning. Crowds? Reporters?

Karen's nimble mind raced ahead.

"You and I should be able to do that. I can get the facts together and you can do the writing. We should do it soon. When are you free?"

"Tomorrow?" Caitlin blurted. She felt dizzy, as if she was tumbling down a long dark passageway, twisting around and around as she floated closer and closer to … she didn't know what.

"Good. We should get this done immediately." Karen nodded in approval. She butted her cigarette against the brick wall of the building with short, brusque jabs. Despite her hair, ghoulish makeup, and blood-red nails, she was businesslike, efficient and very organized. No wonder she and Derek seemed to be a pair, Caitlin thought.

"I'll meet you in the main library in the periodical section. About five. It'll take a couple of hours, so let's count on having dinner there too. Is that your car?" She was looking over Caitlin's shoulder to the streetcar approaching from the west.

It was.

"Tomorrow at five." Karen waved and turned back into the doorway. She was going back to Derek's apartment.

Caitlin climbed thoughtfully onto the streetcar.

Another meeting. What would she tell her mother this time?

11

As it turned out, she only told her half a lie.

Caitlin sighed. Who was she trying to kid? It was a total lie, every word of it.

And she'd said it twice. To her mother. And five minutes ago to Trish.

At first Caitlin had been glad to run into the friendly grade seven student as she walked along the hall outside the science lab.

"Trish. Hey," she'd called out when she glimpsed a flash of red curls in the crowded hall.

"How's that speech coming?" Trish had asked her.

"I'm going to the library right now to do some work on it," Caitlin answered automatically.

The very same lie she had told her mom that morning.

"What library? Here?" Trish had asked.

"No, the big one, in the city. To the periodical section. To see what other newspapers and magazines have said about the role of the press."

Trish had looked impressed.

"No kidding, that'll be great," she had said and left with a friendly wave.

I'll make it be true, Caitlin told herself, running to catch a streetcar into the city. *I'll get there early so I can research the stuff for the Degrassi speech.*

But the streetcar came late and then, after two stops, the driver left everyone sitting as he went into a donut shop to buy some coffee. Then there was a traffic tie-up and the streetcar sat at the same intersection for what seemed like hours. Caitlin looked at her watch. Already 4:30.

When she finally got on the subway, she had only fifteen minutes before she was supposed to meet Karen. She slumped into a seat. No way she'd get any research done on her speech.

Karen was spread out at a table near the magazine racks. There was a stack of newspapers by her left elbow and she was intently reading one of several magazines lying in front of her.

Not looking up, she stuck her hand out on the table in front of her and felt around until she located a felt-tip marker she had laid out.

Caitlin grinned. Today Karen had painted her nails neon orange. On her forefinger she had pasted a phony diamond which reflected in pale coloured shafts when caught by the overhead light.

In the hushed reading area, unrelieved by colour,

Karen's strange black hair and powdered white face might as well have been flashing lights. She was that noticeable.

"Hi." Caitlin slid into the empty chair next to her, pushing aside something heavy, woollenm and black on the table to make room for her knapsack and papers.

"Hey, that's my cloak," Karen squawked, grabbing it and dragging it back.

Across the table, a scholarly man in wire-rimmed glasses looked up from his foreign newspaper and frowned at the girls.

Karen made a face.

"What do you say we go right to the restaurant? We can work on it there."

Without waiting for Caitlin's answer, she swept her black cape over the newspapers and periodicals and walked away from the table.

Caitlin leapt up to follow Karen, hurriedly gathering up the knapsack and bag she had just put down on the table. Then her mouth fell open. Half the pile of newspapers and most of the magazines Karen had been reading had disappeared.

"Whew," Karen slumped against the glass wall of the elevator taking them to the restaurant level. "That was too uptight back there. Here, take these."

From under her cloak she thrust at Caitlin some of the newspapers and magazines she had stealthily taken from the table.

"Aren't we supposed to keep them in the reading area?" Caitlin gasped.

Karen rolled her eyes. "We'll return them, all right?" she said as the elevator doors slid open and she walked swiftly towards the restaurant area. Caitlin scurried after her, balancing her coat, bags, and now newspapers.

With a thud, Karen dumped her cloak and the magazines on a table in the smoking section. "I could use a cigarette," she said. "Now."

Meekly Caitlin dropped into the seat opposite Karen. Her coat and bags slid onto the floor beside her, but she didn't notice. She frowned as she looked at the newspapers she held in her hand. Stolen property.

Karen pushed a blank sheet of paper across the table at Caitlin. "I've got a good idea of what to say now," she said. "But I need a writer to make it sound good."

Caitlin ignored the page.

"What happened last night after I left?" she asked as Karen lit a cigarette.

"Nothing much. I got a few of the articles I knew we'd be needing and left," she answered casually.

"I mean what happened about Derek and ... Robert," Caitlin persisted, keeping her eyes on the table.

The older girl paused and regarded Caitlin with shrewd, amused eyes.

"Oh, that," she said with a wave of her slim arm. "That was just another of Robert's moods. They're buddies again." Karen grinned. "In fact Derek talked Robert into getting his brother's car for them to check out the Darlington site. For the best place for our tent city."

Caitlin's eyes shot up. "And he's doing it?"

Karen smirked. "Of course. Derek can talk anybody into anything."

Caitlin's heart gave a thud. Robert was in it too. They were in it together.

"Caitlin, I thought you were researching your speech."

It was Trish, heading towards her table with a big smile on her friendly face.

Instinctively Caitlin covered the newspapers with her arm. What was Trish doing here? She couldn't sit with them.

"Hi," she muttered through gritted teeth. With her red curly hair and her tasselled pink woollen ski hat, Trish looked just like a kid. *Like a kid my age*, Caitlin reminded herself.

"I figured maybe I could help you with your speech," Trish bubbled. "I want to do some reading on the press, too."

She smiled questioningly at Karen, who was looking at her with a cool gaze, one eyebrow raised slightly. Caitlin remembered that look. It was the one Karen had given her when she had first walked into Derek's. It was a look that took in everything, from the crush socks and Reeboks Trish wore, to the grade seven geography textbook she was carrying.

Inside Caitlin was dying, but she tried to stay cool. She

didn't invite Trish to sit with them; she didn't introduce her to Karen and she didn't look at her.

"I've done it already." Caitlin sounded brusque.

Trish's face fell.

"Oh," she said in a small voice. A silence hung over the three girls.

"So," said Trish. "I'll see you, I guess."

She walked away with slumped shoulders. Biting her lip, Caitlin watched her go.

"Friend of yours?" Karen broke into her thoughts.

"No, no," Caitlin shook her head. "Just a kid who lives on my street. I don't really know her. She's way younger than me."

Karen gave her a calculating look.

Caitlin squirmed in her seat. She knew what the look on Karen's face meant. Trish had blown it for her. Now they would know she was only in junior high school. They'd never let her go to the demo with them.

She fought to keep back the tears. She wanted so much to be with them. She had almost made it, too. It was all Trish's fault.

Karen butted her cigarette.

"So what about you and our Darlington Demo, Caitlin?" she asked, not unkindly.

"What do you mean?" Caitlin replied miserably.

"Well," Karen continued, "the idea is to camp out there overnight for as long as we can last. What are you going to do? There's no way your parents will let you do that, is there?"

Caitlin shook her head unhappily. Karen had hit the nail on the head.

Karen paused. "Do your parents know about this?"

Again Caitlin shook her head, her chin sinking even lower onto her chest.

"Well," Karen sounded crisp, efficient. "This calls for another action plan."

She drummed her long bright nails on the table.

"Why don't you just tell your parents?" she finally said.

Caitlin sat straight up.

"No way," she blurted.

Karen gave the younger girl an exasperated look.

"Look, Caitlin, this is not a bad thing you're doing. Remember that. It's a damn good thing. It's important to make our opinions heard." Karen lit another cigarette. "In fact, it's crucial. People have to know the whole truth about using more nuclear power. Not just the stuff the Hydro people say about providing cheaper and more electricity. But the stuff about the dangers too. And if we don't tell them, who will?"

"You're right," Caitlin burst out. Karen's words had energized her and swept away those doubts that had been gnawing at her. Her eyes glowed as she looked at Karen. Her parents would agree; they just had to.

Across the table, Karen was opening magazines at pages

she had marked and sorting through the newspapers.

"We've got work to do now," she said. "If we don't have any information sheets ready for the press and the people about why we are out there, then there's no point in freezing our butts off in some un-heated tent, is there?"

Caitlin picked up a pen and studied some of the sections in articles Karen had underlined. This was going to be a lot of work.

"If it'll make things easier with your parents, why not try asking them if you can stay at the Tent City just days, not nights, if they're worried?" Karen asked. "Or, after the first day, if they don't want you missing school, you can come out after school for the evenings. Hitch a ride with media or with other people. When people hear what we're doing, they'll start coming out to join us. I'm sure of that."

Caitlin brightened. Maybe, just maybe,0 her parents might go for one of Karen's suggestions.

But Karen wasn't finished. "Either way, Caitlin, you've got to tell them."

She reached across the table and handed Caitlin more newspaper articles. Her dark eyes stared straight into Caitlin's hazel ones. "And tell them the whole thing was your idea. They should be proud of you for thinking of it."

Caitlin smiled wanly at her new friend. If only she could feel as sure about that as Karen did.

Telling her parents was going to be the toughest thing she had ever done.

12

Caitlin snuggled into the couch and shifted the papers on her lap.

On the floor beside her was the pizza box. In it was one greasy slice. Her father usually finished off any left-overs, but this time he had waved it away.

"Dieting," he said, reaching for the evening paper.

Caitlin looked over at him on the recliner. Already he was engrossed in his reading. Her mother was at the kitchen table marking more papers.

It was Friday, the night their family always spent together. She should tell them now.

But first she had to finish her speech. Caitlin glanced at her notes. Mr. Raditch had approved her speech outline that afternoon.

She smiled to herself. He had been in a panic, having forgotten to order enough *Degrassi Digest* sweatshirts so he'd have one to wear onstage too. He was more interested in getting to the phone to order his shirt than in Caitlin's speech.

When Caitlin had left, he was hurrying to the principal's office to phone in an order for one more — extra large. He would pick up the order the next day, and Monday they'd all get their shirts to put on just before the assembly.

"No one should see these until they look up on the stage," he'd scolded, shaking a finger at Caitlin.

Caitlin giggled out loud at the memory. Mr. Raditch was getting a little carried away with this assembly. But it was going to be great. As nervous as she knew she would be, she really wanted to give this speech.

"Laughing to yourself now? You know what that means?" Mr. Ryan had caught her giggle and was peering over the newspaper at her.

Caitlin smiled back at her dad, then twisted around to look at her mother in the kitchen. Maybe now was a good time. She took a deep breath.

"Dad," she said in a high voice.

Her father looked up just as the telephone on the table beside him rang. He picked it up.

"Hello?"

"It's for you," he said.

"Hello," she said into the receiver.

"It's Robert."

His voice was low, close to a whisper. But it was raw and tense with urgency.

"Monday. We have to go Monday."

Caitlin knew her father was watching.

"Oh, hi," she said pleasantly. "Thanks for calling with that information. I was just working on that speech now. But I'm not sure what you mean by that."

For her father's benefit, she rattled some of her pages of notes. He went back to his newspaper.

"Hydro. They've pushed up the start date for the reactor." In the background Caitlin could hear the soundtrack of a movie. He was calling from the store.

"They're starting it Monday. We've got to be there, too."

"Monday?" Caitlin's heart sank. Not Monday. Not *Digest* Day.

"If we don't do it Monday, we don't do it."

She felt a bolt of fear cut through her whole body. She clutched the phone receiver so tightly her knuckles turned white. *Monday, please not Monday.* If she didn't show for the assembly, she would lose her *Digest* job. If she didn't show for the demonstration, she'd lose Robert. And a chance to really make a difference to millions of people.

"We meet tomorrow morning. Derek's at nine." Robert spat out the order.

Caitlin was silent.

"It's crucial we get every detail down then."

Still Caitlin said nothing.

"You'll be there, eh?" Robert sounded less confident now.

She tried to answer but there was a huge lump in her throat blocking her words.

"Caitlin?" Robert finally said. "We need you."

Something in Caitlin broke.

"Okay," she said and hung up the phone.

"Who was that?" her father asked. "Didn't sound like anyone I know."

"A guy," said Caitlin with a sigh. "From the library. With some research."

She fell back on the couch.

"I've got to go to the library tomorrow to get it. Early," she mumbled.

Slowly she picked herself up. Her body felt old and heavy. She jammed the notes for her speech together, not caring whether or not they were in the right order. She wouldn't be needing them. Journalism was over for her now. She wouldn't be giving any speeches as editor of the *Digest*.

Slowly she trudged up the stairs to her room. This was no time to tell her parents.

Outside and one floor below the dingy bow window at 942 Queen Street West, Caitlin stood on the sidewalk. The day was dawning clear and sunny but there were no other people spilling out of doors onto the sidewalk. She was alone.

She looked up again at the window. They were in there, waiting for her. Caitlin squared her shoulders, brushed past the bicycle, and slowly climbed the stairs. Her footsteps sounded heavy. She had made her decision. This — these people — were her choice. She should feel good, but she didn't.

"Hey. Caitlin's here. Now we can get down to business. There's work to do." Derek spotted her hovering in the doorway. Karen and Robert turned and grinned at her.

The atmosphere in the room was crackling with tension. Robert's lean frame seemed poised to spring into action, like a panther about to pounce. Derek's lanky arms chopped the air in rapid, staccato thrusts. Karen's dark eyes were glittering.

The table had been cleared of the piles of newspapers. They'd been thrown into the corner near the couch.

"Won't need them anymore," Robert announced, following her gaze. "We've moved into action, now."

He looked over at Derek and grinned.

The two slapped each others' palms in a high five signal, then pounded each other on the back while Karen good-naturedly rolled her eyes.

"Boys will be boys," she said out of the corner of her mouth to Caitlin, waving her to the chair beside her. Caitlin sank into it. "Is this everybody who is in the demonstration?" she asked hesitantly.

"We may not have the numbers, but we have quality." Derek beamed at her.

"Besides, we'll get the numbers later. After people learn what we are doing. And why," Robert said.

"I mean," Caitlin persisted, feeling stupid but having to know, "did anyone tell Deborah? Did she not want to do it? Did she think it was a stupid idea?"

Karen exchanged looks with Derek. Robert said nothing.

"Deborah dropped out," Derek finally said, as Robert frowned and shifted in his chair.

"She had other priorities," Karen said with a mischievous look at Robert.

Robert scowled. "She didn't really care about nuclear power. She didn't belong here."

Caitlin couldn't help it. She was glad Deborah wasn't coming anymore. She hadn't liked her much. *And not just because Deborah had her eye on Robert, either,* Caitlin told herself. It was a relief not to worry any more about Deborah's bored, haughty looks that made her feel so young and stupid all the time.

"These are fine, just fine," Derek said, holding up the information sheets Caitlin and Karen had pulled together in the library.

"I'm getting copies run off at the library later today. And some folders for the television and newspaper reporters. A real press package," Karen grinned.

Robert was unfolding a detailed map of the area around the Darlington plant. "Here," he said, jabbing a spot next to the highway with his forefinger. "Here is where we set up."

"Close to all amenities. Nuclear included," Karen

joked. "Did you go out and check out the scene?"

"We did. After he got off work." Derek ducked his head towards Robert.

"So," Karen continued. "It was a dark and stormy night. But our heroes ventured forth nonetheless. And when you arrived, you fought through howling winds and blinding snowstorms —"

"Fraid not. Black skies only. Lit by the passing headlights of cars speeding by on one of our nation's finest highways to points east," Derek grinned.

"Maybe to infinity," Robert chimed in.

"You went out to the Darlington nuclear site?" Caitlin asked incredulously.

"Indeed. We came. We saw —" Derek began.

"We shook our fists." Robert finished off Derek's thought.

"And thumbed our noses," a grinning Derek one-upped him.

"And after you finished acting like eleven-year-olds, you checked out the site?" Karen asked. She was smiling.

Robert calmed down. "Absolutely," he answered. "We found just the right spot for our protest site."

"Near the highway. The cars will have a great view of us." Derek added.

"Otherwise it's out of sight, out of mind," Caitlin said.

Robert gave her an appreciative look. "Exactly. People have to see us. Otherwise why do it?"

"I mean, suppose you threw a protest and nobody came?" Caitlin spoke up again, emboldened by his look.

Derek's smile widened. "Caitlin's got the point. People will see our banners from the highway. They'll see our tents from the highway. Maybe just four of them now, but soon there will be rows and rows of them, filled with people who don't want to live with the dangers of nuclear power." He pushed back his chair and paced back and forth across the room. "Soon everyone will know about our Tent City. They'll see it on television, in the papers —"

"And they'll know the spirit of the Greenham Common women lives on — here in Canada," Caitlin burst in, carried away by the picture his words created for her. It was going to be wonderful. And important. And they would change things.

Under the table she squeezed her hands tightly together. She had made the right choice.

"And before we go, we'll send press kits to all the reporters so they know," Caitlin said, watching Karen carefully remove orange nail polish from her right hand.

"That's the plan," Robert said, with a glance at Derek. It was a smug look which Karen didn't see and Caitlin didn't understand.

Karen was now concentrating on applying a coat of garish purple polish to her right thumbnail.

"You're getting that friend of your's car, right?" Robert asked her. The girl nodded and dipped her brush into the polish. "Well, you could drop off press kits before heading out to Darlington, couldn't you?"

"Caitlin, you'll help out Karen," Derek said. "The reporters would probably trust someone who looks like you more than someone like me —"

"Who looks like an unmade bed," Robert cut in.

"Or, for sure, someone who wears his hair in a pony-tail." Derek made a face at his friend. "Robert and I should go straight to the site. We want to get the tents and a ban-ner up while there's still morning traffic. Karen will drive you around and then get you out to the site."

Robert was nodding enthusiastically.

"Yeah, it'll work out just right," he said.

Karen was nodding her head as if they were arranging to meet for a hamburger, Caitlin realized. Was she the only one who still had butterflies in her stomach? Weren't they even a little bit worried? She was, even though it was all very exciting. She was nervous, too. And, deep down, scared, really scared.

She looked over at the others. Robert's blue eyes were blazing with excitement. She had never seen him look so handsome, or so powerful. He was a different person from the quiet, gentle clerk she had talked to in the video store.

And Karen. Caitlin's gaze fell on the dark head of the girl, bent over painting her nails. She had been so friendly and nice at the library, but Caitlin didn't really know her.

She didn't really know any of them. Could she trust

them? Was this the right thing to be doing?

It is, Caitlin told herself, *of course it is.* But her head was filling with doubts that wouldn't go away. Why did so many plans get made when she wasn't around? And did Derek and Robert really know what they were doing? Why were they acting so stupid, fooling around so much? Weren't they taking this seriously? Caitlin bit her lip. If this was the beginning of a Tent City, why weren't they organizing for a long stay? Shouldn't they be telling other groups who were also against nuclear power? And the organizations against nuclear weapons? Wouldn't they want to know? Maybe be part of the Tent City?

And the women of Greenham Common had been camping for years. Shouldn't they be thinking about food and water and how to stay warm, not just press releases?

"I'll deliver the press releases, but —" she began.

"Good." Derek nodded. "That's the important thing."

He had not looked up from the map. Nobody noticed she was upset. Robert and Derek weren't paying attention to anyone except each other. Karen, looking up from her nails, frowned in the direction of the boys. They weren't paying much attention to her, either.

Suddenly Caitlin felt sad. She could walk out of the room and no one would notice, she told herself. On Monday she would give her speech about the *Digest* and the importance of newspapers instead.

Caitlin sat up straighter. Or would she? What was more

important, really? She couldn't walk away now. Not after all she'd been through. Not when the day of the demonstration was so close.

Derek folded away the map and turned around to face Caitlin and Karen. "Caitlin, you and Robert get started on a banner. The paint and sheet are over beside the couch."

Shyly, Caitlin turned to look at Robert, who was already getting up from the table. He walked over to her chair and lightly touched her shoulder. "Come on, I'll need some help on this." Caitlin rose and followed him, her shoulder tingling where his hand had been. He sank into the dusty sofa and patted the cushion next to him. She was to sit there.

The skin on her neck prickled; she could feel a flush cover her face as she dropped down beside him.

"You got some idea of what to put on the banner?" Robert asked, stretching back and resting one arm on top of the couch behind Caitlin's head.

Caitlin's head was spinning. It was hard to think; it was hard to breathe.

"It should have our name on it —" she began.

"Name? What name?" Robert sounded a little annoyed.

"Darlington Common. In honour of the Greenham Common women who kept the vigil," Caitlin replied hesitantly. It was the first thing that sprang into her head. She knew he would think it was stupid. But she was nervous. He was too close to her.

Robert didn't reply.

"We could call it something else," Caitlin stammered. "We could —"

"No." Robert stopped her. His voice was gentle now. "You've got it. That's exactly what we must say. It shows honour and respect and that their cause is our cause."

There was a pause as he, too, sat forward on the couch. He took one of Caitlin's clenched hands. "It's perfect. Thanks."

Still holding her hand, he stood up, pulling her up too. Robert looked down at her, then over at the paint and brushes. "Let's do it," he said.

Caitlin couldn't look at him, but inside she was shaking with uncontrollable joy. Keeping her eyes from him, she began to spread out the bedsheet someone had brought to the apartment. Robert was prying open the paint tin and mixing the deep green paint with a stick.

"Figure out how many letters that is and how much space we have," he called over to her.

Caitlin nodded happily. He liked her idea. Maybe he liked her. And he did care about the demonstration. She knew that now.

Just under an hour later, the banner was finished and drying over most of the meeting room floor. The newly named Darlington Common was spelled out in letters two feet high.

"A work of art," Karen pronounced, as the four of

them stood in a line admiring it.

"Yeah," Robert laughed, taking a swipe at a streak of green on the side of Caitlin's nose with a rag soaked with paint remover. Caitlin squealed and ducked.

Derek frowned and went back to the table. "Let's get back to basics now," he commanded, as the other three meekly filed back and sat down.

Derek consulted the top sheet on a pad of yellow legal paper on which he had made a list.

"Robert, you're bringing the water and some firewood. Karen, you're getting the campfire gear from your parents. Caitlin, just get that tent of yours —"

"Tent?" Caitlin gulped. She was abruptly brought back to reality.

"You said you have a tent. Didn't you?" Derek swung around and stared at her coldly.

"Yes, but it's not mine. It's my dad's," she whispered.

"So?"

"So it's not mine."

"So," Derek repeated. "Take it anyway."

"You mean steal it?" Caitlin said. Her stomach knotted.

Derek looked at her coolly.

"Whatever it takes," he said. "That's how we do things here."

13

Six o'clock. Caitlin sat straight up in bed. Her heart was racing, her eyes wide open.

In exactly two hours Karen would be here. Then they would drop off the press kits at two television stations — one in the centre of the city, the other in the outskirts — on their way to Darlington.

Then — Caitlin bit her lip — then they would go to Darlington.

Caitlin looked at the clock again. 6:12. Her mother should be getting up now and her father would be rising as soon as Caitlin's mom was finished in the bathroom. They always left for work at 7:45, ten minutes to eight at the absolute latest.

That would give her ten minutes to collect the tent and sleeping bag before Karen was due.

Caitlin shivered. What if her parents were late just this one morning? What if Karen was early?

She could hear the shower now. 6:15. Her mother was

right on schedule. Relax, she told herself. Everything will go off without a hitch. They had everything.

Caitlin hugged her knees and burrowed into the comforter for warmth. She knew she wasn't cold. She was scared.

What Derek and Robert didn't know, what Karen didn't know, what nobody knew, was that Caitlin hadn't told anybody about this. Not her parents. No one. Only Robert, Derek, and Karen knew where she would be today. If anything happened to her — Caitlin rubbed her eyes. She mustn't think like that. No wonder she had barely slept last night.

The minute Mr. Raditch realized she was a no-show for the *Digest* assembly he'd have the school secretary on the phone to her parents. Then what?

She jumped out of the bed. In twenty minutes Robert and Derek would be on their way to Darlington. In ninety minutes Karen would drive up in her friend's old Honda. Caitlin ran to the window. It looked cold and dark out there. Layers — she would need layers of clothes to make it through this day.

She pulled thermal underwear over her head, shaking her hair free, then a black turtleneck sweater, and finally her pink baggy sweatsuit. She'd need a scarf along with hat and mittens; she'd look after that when her parents had gone. No use doing anything that would make them question her today.

Abruptly Caitlin peeled off her layers. They might suspect something. She would put on the extra clothes when they left. If she moved fast there would be enough time. She went to her closet and picked out a navy dress she often wore, and her silver belt.

"Are you going to be warm enough today?" her mother asked, looking at Caitlin's thin knit dress.

"I'm wearing a sweater over it," Caitlin mumbled, staring down at her bowl of muesli. Her stomach was in knots. She couldn't eat, but she knew she had to. It would be cold out there at Darlington.

Her mother ruffled her hair as she passed by the back of Caitlin's chair. Her father didn't look up from his newspaper.

It seemed hours before they both raced out the door, her mother loaded with her bulging briefcase of marked papers, her father with his tennis bag.

"Bye," Caitlin waved cheerfully. But every muscle in her body strained for the sound of two cars backing out of the driveway. She sat tense and coiled. Had they gone? Yes. She ran downstairs for the tent and then upstairs to change her clothes.

She was wrapping a scarf around her neck when she heard a car honk. Caitlin looked at her watch. Karen was right on time.

She threw on her camelhair duffle coat, grabbed the tent, and ran outside. She was so nervous she fumbled trying to open the car door. Karen made a face and leaned over the front seat to open the door for Caitlin.

"Thanks, I'm a bit jittery," Caitlin said nervously as she threw her tent in the back seat.

"Don't know why that would be," the older girl answered laconically.

Caitlin looked at Karen. She had on a black woollen hat pulled low over her head, covering all her hair and making her face look even paler. Its toque was so long it went half way down her back. The pompom on it was in Day-Glo orange. So were her gloves. Everything else was pitch-black — everything except her bright orange lipstick. Karen had amazing flair, even now, Caitlin thought.

"Shhhhh," Karen said backing out of the driveway. She was listening to an FM radio station. "I like this song."

Caitlin sat in silence. How could Karen be so cool?

"Got the flyers?" Caitlin asked when the song was over.

Karen pointed to the back seat, then lit a cigarette.

"Bring the banner?" Caitlin asked a few minutes later.

Karen exhaled. "Relax, kid. It's all together. Now sit back and listen to the music. The radio's the only thing that works in this car."

She steered into the morning rush-hour traffic. The roads were jammed.

What if they got stuck in traffic? What if they were late?

"We've got tons of time," said Karen. "When we get on the highway, we'll be going against most of the traffic."

Karen was right. Within twenty minutes they had

dropped off the press kit to the first television station and were heading onto Highway 401.

"Right on schedule," Karen said. "Now sit back and enjoy this if you can."

Impossible, Caitlin thought, sitting tense in the cold little car. Her teeth chattered as much from nerves as from the chill in the air.

Karen wheeled off the highway towards the second television station.

"Stay put," she ordered, picking up a kit and heading through the wide front doors. Seconds later she was back.

They rode in silence until Caitlin saw the sign marking Exit 428.

"That's us," she said. Her voice was wobbly. The knot in her stomach tightened even more. Her heart beat a pattern so loud she was sure Karen could hear it.

If only they could turn back. What was she doing here? This was all a horrible mistake.

"Keep an eye out for the guys. See if you can see them from the road," said Karen. "Their tents are supposed to be near the highway so we should be able to spot them."

Steady, Caitlin told herself, trying to breathe deeply. *Calm down. It's going to be all right.* She caught sight of a flash of blue and green over to her right. Tents.

"There they are," Caitlin said. Her voice was shaky.

Derek and Robert had pitched one tent on the north side of the road and the other tent a short distance away on the other side of the road. That was so the banner announcing Darlington Common that Caitlin and Robert had painted on Saturday could be read from the highway — it hung between the two tents.

Karen groaned. In front of the campsite, parked off the sideroad, was the mud-spattered brown van Robert had borrowed from his brother. And behind it, in a row, three Ontario Hydro pick-up trucks.

Caitlin's heart leapt into her mouth.

Karen stubbed out her cigarette. "Damn. Security has spotted them already. For God's sake, look innocent as we go by. Pretend we don't know them."

She slowly drove along the turnoff, until she seemed to be headed straight for the guardhouse and the barbed wire fence marking Gate 2 of the Darlington nuclear plant.

To their left was a huge billboard. Caitlin shrank as she read it: "No trespassing. Authorized personnel only. All others must report to the security guardhouse"

More rules in smaller print followed. "Eye protection must be worn on the site." "Vehicles or persons entering or leaving will be searched." "Ontario Hydro assumes no responsibility for loss or damage to vehicles or contents, however caused"

Karen turned the car away from the forbidding entrance and headed down the service road that ran alongside the highway. This was the road where Robert and Derek had pitched their tents.

Karen took her foot off the gas. "Okay, Caitlin, now you'd better start acting as if your life depended on it," she snapped. "We have things we have to do, even if the guys have messed up."

Caitlin swallowed. What had happened? What had gone wrong? Couldn't Derek and Robert pitch their tents anyway, just like the women in Greenham Common? The land didn't belong to the company. They couldn't do anything.

Karen slowed down as they drove closer to the tents. Three security guards were with Robert and Derek. One was speaking into a walkie-talkie he held in his hand. A second guard was starting to take down the tents. The other had already pulled down the banner.

The security guards looked up as they heard the car approach. One of them stepped onto the road and gestured for Karen to keep driving.

Robert's eyes met Caitlin's. The security guard had his back to him. "Go for it," Robert mouthed.

Caitlin squared her shoulders, pretended to look puzzled for the sake of the guards. She peered, frowned; she turned around in her seat to get a last look.

"Don't get carried away, kid," Karen said.

Caitlin fell back in her seat. "I don't get it," she said. "Why did the guards stop the guys? They can't do that."

Karen gripped the steering wheel. "Oh, yes, they can. This road must belong to Ontario Hydro. I was pretty sure it did," she said, more to herself than to Caitlin. "I told

Derek. He said he'd check, but obviously he didn't."

"So what if Ontario Hydro owns it?" Caitlin said.

"So what?" Karen repeated, her voice rising. "That means we're on private property. That means they can throw us out of here. Legally. So much for our tent city. The women of Greenham Common are outside the military base. On public land."

Karen pulled up into the parking lot near the Information Centre. It was 9:45 a.m. In another fifteen minutes a tour would start. They could hand out some pamphlets then.

She stopped the car, then pounded the steering wheel.

"Damn," she said. "Why'd they have to do it there? Why'd they have to get caught?"

"What do we do now?" Caitlin asked in a small voice. She felt lost and she was afraid. No one had said anything about security guards.

"I don't know," Karen replied. "But we're not giving up, get that?"

She peered through the windshield, talking more to herself than to Caitlin. "We should get at least one banner up. Maybe a tent, too, before the cameras get here."

"Cameras?" Caitlin asked. "What cameras?"

Karen ignored her question. "That's probably the best spot back there," she said to herself.

Getting out of the car, she said over her shoulder to Caitlin, "You grab the information sheets in the back and cover the entrance to the Information Centre."

But Caitlin sat in the car. She was shaking with fear. Outside, the northwest wind howled through the parking lot. She looked around. Four cars, one mini-van. Bleak, desolate, empty. There was no one about. And no one knew she was here.

Caitlin dug around in the back seat for the flyers. She had to do something; Robert was counting on her. She'd put the sheets inside the Information Centre.

As she slipped out of the car, the wind flung her beige scarf against her frightened face. The sky was steel-grey, oppressive, cold. The wind howled as it whipped around corners; otherwise, there was silence. Picnic tables were stacked on their sides waiting for the return of good weather. Behind her was a baseball diamond.

The wind stung her face as she crept towards the Information Centre, an ordinary one-storey building. Caitlin's heart was racing. Although it was cold, the palms of her hands were sweaty. South of the centre, down the cliff dropping to the lake, she glimpsed the power station itself: sleek, windowless, and the same foreboding grey as the sky.

That was where the reactors were. And the facilities for storing the tritium. Yet it looked strong and safe, stark against the cold, dark waters of the lake. One article she had read said that people who live within eight kilometres of a nuclear power plant have the same chance of getting cancer as they do getting of cirrhosis of the liver from drinking two glasses of wine.

Could it be true? Caitlin halted. No, she couldn't consider that now. She had done the research; she believed nuclear power was never safe. What would happen if there were ever an accident here?

She shuddered, but this time not from the cold. They had to do this. People must know of this danger; they must understand.

She searched the far end of the parking lot for Karen. A flash of orange caught the corner of her eye. It was Karen waving from over at the baseball diamond.

Caitlin gasped. Karen had hung a banner on the baseball fence. "Tritium: A bitter spill to swallow" could be read by anybody walking out of the Information Centre.

Karen was pointing at her now, waving even more animatedly. Caitlin turned around. The first tour was leaving the centre. People were walking towards the mini-van.

Without thinking, Caitlin ran towards them, waving her flyers. They stared, quickening their pace to reach the van before her. A few stopped long enough to read Karen's banner.

A yellow school bus turned into the parking lot and pulled to a stop near the entrance. Behind steamed windows, students about Caitlin's age peered at the banner, then at her.

Some pointed, others laughed as they stepped in single

file out of the bus. A tall, tense man in horn-rimmed glasses planted himself in front of Caitlin and tersely ordered the students to hurry along. Most did as they were told, but two girls stopped and took an information sheet from Caitlin.

"What's tritium?" one of them asked.

"Don't talk to her," shouted the teacher. He turned and snatched a flyer from Caitlin's hand. Glaring at her, he marched over to the centre and handed it to a Darlington tour guide standing just inside the doorway.

Caitlin couldn't hear what he was saying but she saw the teacher point to her. The tour guide quickly disappeared from view.

Caitlin was stung. They treated her as if she were a leper. What had ever happened to freedom of speech?

"Hey," she called out to the last of the students and to the hostile teacher who was quickly shepherding them into the building. "What's the matter? Afraid to learn the truth of what goes on here?"

The door closed behind them. Caitlin took a step towards it, then stopped. It was probably not a good time to go in and leave flyers inside the Centre. Better wait until she was sure that class — and their creepy teacher — were settled in the auditorium with the doors closed, watching the movie and hearing the tour lecture.

She looked back towards the baseball field to find Karen. She saw her, a dramatic figure in black bent against the wind, making her way across the parking lot towards her. Karen couldn't see one of the Hydro security trucks careening into the parking lot at breakneck speed. Or the police car that was right behind it.

They screeched to a stop. Two men jumped out of each vehicle and ran towards Caitlin.

14

Caitlin sat with her back against the pale yellow cinder-block wall. She could have been in a principal's office, but she wasn't. She was in the Bowmanville police station and she was under arrest.

It was so hot. She had been sitting in this ugly room for hours. She had on all those layers of clothes — they smelled of the smoke from Karen's cigarettes, and Caitlin felt trapped in them, as if she couldn't move. Why didn't the police just let them go?

What were they doing, anyway? They had her mother's and father's phone numbers. They had her name, age, school. Why was she still here?

Robert had been no comfort. All he had done since the arrest was pace the room demanding his rights.

"I want those guards charged with harassment," he said.

"Good luck," Derek answered sarcastically. He looked at Karen sitting next to him on the bench against the wall.

"Robert, I told you, we goofed. That land we put the tents on belongs to Hydro. We were trespassing," Karen said, with a sigh. They had been through this before. "They've got us."

"Not when my lawyer gets here," Robert retorted. He was like a caged animal.

"Did you notice one thing?" Derek said with a laugh. "They didn't take down Karen's sign on the ball park." He smiled at her. "That was good thinking, to put the sign up there and not near the tents."

"Probably gone now," Karen said gruffly, but she couldn't help grinning at Derek's praise.

"This is a mess," Caitlin finally said in a shaky voice. She didn't think she could hold back the tears another moment.

"No, it isn't." Robert snapped out the words. "It is NOT a mess and it is NOT over. The fight is just beginning."

Derek turned to Caitlin. "Robert's right. As soon as we're out of here, I'm going to the papers with the news of our arrest. Now we've got the story we wanted to happen."

Karen beamed at him. "Yeah, but you are getting way too efficient, Derek. You figured we'd be in the tents for a day. We didn't even make it for an hour."

Dumbfounded, Caitlin stared at Karen, watching her laugh and squeeze Derek's arm.

Even Robert smiled. "That was long enough, thanks. It

was cold out there at seven this morning. I would have frozen to death sleeping in tents. I never thought that was such a smart idea."

"Who did?" Derek asked, with a grin.

"Well, if you remember, I did — at least until you guys explained to me the plan you two cooked up when you were casing Darlington," Karen giggled.

Caitlin gaped at the three of them. They had lied to her, led her on. They had never planned on starting a Tent City that would last, after all. They had just wanted to put up tents long enough for the television news cameras to film it. They had planned on a one-day-long protest.

Caitlin thought about the Greenham Common women, who had been faithful to their cause for years and years. She felt as if she had been hit in the stomach.

Robert finally noticed Caitlin's face.

"Hey, didn't you know?" he asked carelessly. "No, that's right. We figured you'd hold out for overnights so we didn't tell you, did we?"

He dropped himself down on the bench beside her. Caitlin shifted away from him.

"We haven't changed our stand on nuclear energy, you know," he protested as Caitlin turned her head away from him.

Karen wasn't paying attention to them. Since they had been detained, her dark eyes had stayed focused on Derek.

"If this gets covered in the papers — or even better, on

the television — you'll become one of the leaders of all the anti-nuclear groups," she said to him now. "You'll be able to get all the groups together and really make a difference."

Derek looked pleased. So, Caitlin saw, did Robert.

And Karen was content, just to be sitting shoulder-to-shoulder next to Derek.

Not me, Caitlin thought suddenly. *I didn't want this. I don't want my name in the paper, please no. Not this way.*

"Do you have to tell the press?" she pleaded to Derek.

He looked at her scornfully. "What's come over you? Of course, we go to the media. You should know that. Otherwise, what's the point of going through all this?" His long arm indicated the stark room they were sitting in.

"But you never said you'd do this," Caitlin wailed.

Derek let out an exasperated sigh. "I can't believe how naive you are. Without the press, who is going to know what we did today, except for a few people on a tour of Darlington? We've got to get the message about the danger of tritium out."

"Even if the demonstration didn't exactly go our way," Karen added.

Derek nodded emphatically as all the life seemed to drain from Caitlin. She felt used, and used up, and very, very tired.

The door flew open and Caitlin's mother rushed in. She ran straight to Caitlin, bent down and wrapped her arms around her.

"It's okay, it's okay," she murmured.

Caitlin collapsed in her mother's strong embrace. She was going home now. Thank goodness her mother had come.

"Hi, Mom," she said weakly. "I'm glad you're here."

They walked past the stern-faced policeman who had followed her mother into the room. Caitlin's mother nodded to him as he held the door open for them.

Outside they crossed the parking lot to her mother's car. Caitlin sank into the soft seat and pulled on her seatbelt.

Her mother slid in behind the wheel, patted Caitlin on the shoulder, and turned the ignition key. The sound of the radio filled the car. Caitlin leaned back on the headrest and closed her eyes.

She would have to tell them the whole story, she knew that. But right now, all she wanted was to go home.

Her mother wheeled the car onto the highway. They were halfway to Toronto before Caitlin remembered something.

She had not said goodbye to the others.

"So," said her father, settling himself on the couch, "tell me everything you know about tritium."

"Rob, this is no time for jokes," Caitlin's mother said sharply.

But Caitlin smiled at her father. Thank goodness he

was teasing her. Her mother hadn't said very much driving home. Not that she had been angry, it wasn't that. More like thoughtful.

That afternoon, lying on her bed, Caitlin had heard her mother call the school and talk to the principal, Mr. Lawrence, and to Mr. Raditch. Caitlin had got up and closed her door so she wouldn't overhear any of that call. She had skipped the assembly, the most important assembly ever for the *Digest*. And for what?

Her father had come home right after school, and had gone straight into the dining room with her mother. They'd closed the double doors and talked in there for a long time.

But now it was time for her to talk. To come clean. Caitlin took a deep breath. Funny, now she wanted to tell them everything.

"Okay if I start right at the very beginning?" she asked.

Her mother nodded.

So Caitlin told them about meeting Robert and about bringing the movie *If You Love This Planet* home to watch.

"You watched it here? I don't remember that," her father interrupted.

"Rob, you were probably out and I was probably working," Caitlin's mother cut in. Then, turning to Caitlin, she added, "We saw that movie, too, but quite a few years ago when it first came out. When you were still pretty little."

Her parents had seen the movie; they might have understood how she felt. Caitlin gazed in amazement from her mother to her father. She could have talked to them all along. Maybe she needn't have told them all those lies.

"I'm not proud of this," she continued and told them about lying about studying with Joey and doing research at the library, and instead going to Derek's. She started to tell them about what she had learned there, but her father broke into her story.

"How old did you say these kids were?" he asked. His mouth was set in a firm line and his voice was harsh. "And what were you doing in a boy's apartment on your own?"

"I was never on my own there, Daddy. Nothing ever happened there. Nothing like that, anyway," Caitlin protested, worried because she could see how angry her father was becoming. "I was learning things there."

Her mother looked thoughtful. "You know, Rob," she said. "It's not as if our daughter was caught stealing or even doing drugs. Caitlin obviously thought a lot about it. She just got very serious about something that was very serious."

Mr. Ryan was still scowling.

"She knows more about tritium than I do — my own daughter," Caitlin's mother continued. "And I'm beginning to think I should know something about what is going on so close to us, too."

"She broke the law, not to mention she snuck around behind our backs for weeks. I don't like it," Caitlin's father snapped.

She had broken the law, Caitlin knew that now. She

had trespassed on private property. But she had never even considered that as a possibility when she was thinking about doing something in a small way to honour the courageous women of Greenham Common.

She hadn't thought it through enough. She had been too impulsive. It had started right and ended wrong. She knew she had been right to question the increasing use of nuclear power — especially so close to where she lived.

But who would believe her now or even listen to her? Would they remember that she had cared enough to take a stand? No way; they'd only remember that Caitlin Ryan has a police record.

Now she would probably never get a job when she was older. Who would hire a convicted criminal?

Her mother looked over and smiled gently at Caitlin's woebegone face.

"I'm not excusing what you did or the fact that we didn't know anything about your activities," she said. "But, Caitlin, stop looking as if this is the end of the world. It's not. Your life will go on."

Caitlin said miserably, "I've been charged. I've broken the law. Nobody will ever talk to me again."

Her parents exchanged a look.

Her father cleared his throat. "I'm pretty sure they're going to drop the charges against you," he said.

Caitlin sat straight up. Drop the charges? That meant no record; she'd be clear.

"Your two friends aren't so lucky. Charges of mischief are pending against them," her father continued in a stern voice. "That's because Hydro figures that banner they set up between the two tents was obstructing the road. Depending on how things go, your friends could get six months in jail or a fine of up to $2,000."

Caitlin cringed.

"What about Karen?" she asked.

"Is she the girl who put up the banner on the baseball field? She'll probably get off. The people at Hydro weren't too concerned about that. Or about you and your pamphlets. They've known one or two protesters before," her father said.

Her mother interrupted him. "You're lucky you're only turning fourteen. That makes you a Young Offender under the law, and even if they do charge you, you'll probably get a suspended sentence."

"And my name in the paper. Terrific. I might as well be convicted," Caitlin said.

Again her parents looked at each other.

"Well, looks like I've got more good news for you," her father said. "The media can't report the names of Young Offenders charged with a crime."

"Great, that means nobody at Degrassi has to know," Caitlin cried. Her forehead creased as she started trying to think of some excuse she'd tell them about why she missed the assembly.

Her parents exchanged a look.

"Caitlin ...," her mother started to say.

The telephone rang.

"I'll get it," her father said, getting up to take the call on the phone in the hallway.

Her mother continued. "Caitlin, I've told the principal and I've talked with Mr. Raditch. They know. You should be honest with your friends —"

She stopped and looked up at Caitlin's father standing in the doorway.

"Caitlin, it's Melanie," he said. "She wants to know why you weren't at school today. Are you going to take the call?"

Caitlin looked over at her mother. "Oh, no, please," she begged.

"I think you should," her mother replied.

Caitlin let out a deep sigh and got up to answer the phone.

She paused in the doorway.

"I guess you're right," she said with a sad smile. "I guess I have to start telling the truth sometime."

15

"Do I have to?"

Mrs. Ryan looked at Caitlin's pale, tired face and hugged her daughter.

"Yes. You have to go to school. Face up to it. Get it over and done with."

It had been a terrible night, Caitlin's second in a row with no sleep. First excitement, now fear kept her awake. Fear of going to back to Degrassi. Facing Mr. Raditch, Trish, the others at the *Digest*. She had let them all down.

Her father burst into the kitchen. Three newspapers were under his arm.

"Well, my girl," he said cheerfully. "You made two out of three. Not the front page, mind you. In fact, you might say it's buried in the back pages. But at least you made the papers."

"But you said they couldn't use my name," Caitlin cried, feeling the tears starting.

Her father smiled at her. "Sorry. Bad time to tease.

.They didn't. You are referred to as, ahem, a 'female minor.'"

Caitlin managed a wan smile. But she peered at the papers over her father's shoulder.

"What does it say? Where's the story?"

"Here." Her father tapped a story in the paper with the headline "Top scholar arrested in tritium protest."

"Who is this Robert Tertiani? He seems to have some strong opinions on the subject," he commented.

Caitlin peered at the story. "He's the guy who works at the Big Seen. I told you about him last night."

"The guy in the video store?" Her father sounded surprised. "Well, he's bright enough. It says here he was the top grade thirteen scholar in the province last year. But you say he works in a video store?"

"Just for this year. He's going to university next year."

Mr. Ryan put down the paper. "I put in a call to Mr. Pasquill last night after you went to bed. He's our family lawyer. I want you to see him. He says Thursday after school is a good time."

Caitlin stiffened. "Why do I need a lawyer? You said I was okay. You said I wouldn't be charged with anything."

Her mother spoke in a soothing voice. "You don't need a lawyer. This is just to be on the safe side. It doesn't mean anything. Now come on and I'll drive you to school."

Reluctantly Caitlin went to collect her books and coat. They weren't going to let her get away with anything. A lawyer. And an escort right to the door of the school.

At least she was early. Darting through the empty halls, Caitlin went directly to the only hide-out she could think of — the cramped *Digest* office.

One *Digest* sweatshirt was lying on the table. Caitlin stroked the soft blue material. That was her sweatshirt, the one she was supposed to wear yesterday for the speech.

She sat down and picked up a pencil, then she reached for a piece of paper. Maybe there was one last article she could write.

She frowned, collecting her thoughts.

The office door flew open and crashed against the bookcase. Caitlin's head shot up. Joey was standing in the doorway.

"So, I hear you're a jailbird," he grinned.

Darn that Melanie. Of course, she had told Snake everything and he would tell Joey. Now everyone would know.

She took a deep breath.

"It's not something I'm proud of," she said steadily.

Joey sat in the chair opposite her and he took off his hat. "Pretty gutsy, though," he said.

"Who? What?"

"You. Going to that nuclear place. Planning all that. With those other people." Joey took a deep breath. "That was that guy in the video store, right?"

Caitlin nodded.

"What was with him, anyway?"

Caitlin felt her temper start to flare. How dare he ask all these questions. It was none of his business. With a furious look, she bent back to what she had been writing.

A silence fell over the room, but Joey still sat there.

Exasperated, Caitlin put down her pencil again.

"More to the point," she said to Joey curtly, "what's with you, anyway? I don't have to explain anything to you."

Joey hung his head. "I'm sorry," he mumbled. "I guess I should have said I was wrong about him. And him and you, I mean. That's why I went to the dance with Liz."

Caitlin's anger disappeared. "I have to apologize to you, too, Joey. I lied to you about why I wasn't studying with you."

She forced herself to go on. "I hated telling all those lies. I felt really bad."

Joey reached for his hat. "You did?" he exclaimed.

"Yeah."

Joey pushed back his chair and stood up.

"So, maybe you'll ... we'll ... I mean, at the next dance. Christmas. I mean, we'll go together then. Really this time, I mean."

Caitlin looked up at Joey. He wanted a second chance. Just like her.

"Sure," she said.

He grinned and bounded out the door.

Caitlin retrieved the piece of paper and began writing.

She was chewing the end of the pencil thoughtfully when Mr. Raditch poked his head around the door.

"I hear you had a busy day yesterday," he said, perching himself on the table in front of her.

"I'm sorry. Did my mother tell you?" she asked.

Mr. Raditch nodded.

"I really wanted to give that speech. I had the notes made and everything, and then they called and told me the demonstration had to be yesterday. I didn't know until Friday night, honest." Caitlin hung her head. "I'm sorry I let you down."

Mr. Raditch cleared his throat.

"The show did go on, though. I was the pinch-hitter. Speech was pretty good, too, if I do say so."

Caitlin looked up. Mr. Raditch was smiling.

"It wasn't the end of the world, as it turned out," he said suddenly. "Which I gather is what you had in mind to protest when you chose to go to the nuclear power station instead of coming to school yesterday."

A look or horror crossed Caitlin's face. How could he joke about this?

"Tritium isn't funny; it might be very dangerous," she burst out, then bit her lip. She had blown it again.

But Mr. Raditch was still smiling.

"I understand your concern," he said. "And your respect for those women at Greenham Common. They were your role models, I gather?"

"I ... we ... wanted to honour them," she replied.

Mr. Raditch raised his eyebrow. "And so you should. They were very brave women to camp outside that base for all those years. In winter, in the rain, without water, without anything. All because they believed there should be no nuclear missiles in the world."

Caitlin was too surprised to say anything. So Mr. Raditch knew about the Greenham Common women, too.

"I was arrested once," he said suddenly.

"You were?" Caitlin gasped.

Mr. Raditch nodded. "In university. We found out the university had shares in a huge company that manufactured some of the weapons they were using in Viet Nam. In the war there. I know what it's like to believe in something. What I had forgotten was kids these days believe in things too."

He picked up the sweatshirt. "School dances are important. But they're not everything."

He turned and looked at her. "So, can the editor come up with a nice mix for the next issue? A little controversy, maybe an opinion or two? Even the facts on both sides of an issue?"

Caitlin felt a surge of happiness run through her.

She beamed at the teacher, who had moved to the door.

"I'll leave you to your writing," he said.

"It's something for the *Digest*," Caitlin answered, stammering slightly. "I mean, maybe you'll want it."

"I'll look at it when it's finished," he said crisply. "An issue piece, I presume?"

Firmly he closed the door. Caitlin looked down at the words she'd written on the page so far.

> Yesterday I was arrested. I learned a lot from this. I learned that sometimes bad things come from good causes. But that does not mean the cause is not still good.

That's not a bad beginning for something this hard to write, she thought. It wasn't always easy getting at the truth. But it was what journalists were supposed to do.

She smiled to herself. This was one story she really wanted to do.

Caitlin picked up the chewed pencil and bent down to write some more.

About the Author

Catherine Dunphy is the author of BLT, another novel in Lorimer's classic Degrassi Junior High series. A feature writer for The Toronto Star, she is also the author of Morgentaler, A Difficult Hero, shortlisted for a Governor General's Literary Award, and she has written for television, radio, and magazines.

More books in the Degrassi Junior High Series...

Joey Jeremiah

By Kathryn Ellis

Joey Jeremiah is going to be a rock star. He's sure his band, Zit Remedy, is going to go all the way and bring him the fame and fortune he deserves. Then Joey fails grade eight. He's shocked, embarrassed, and scared-until he spots an ad for a Battle of the Bands. If Zit Remedy wins, this could be Joey's chance to show he's still headed for big things, after all.

$9.95

ISBN10 1-55028-924-1
ISBN13 978-1-55028-924-4

More books in the Degrassi Junior High Series...

Snake

By Susin Nielsen

Grade nine isn't turning out the way Snake planned. He made the basketball team, but the captain wants to get him booted off. The prettiest girl at Degrassi thinks he's a geek, his marks are falling, and his brother has announced that he's gay. Can Snake get it together before the year becomes a total disaster?

$9.95

ISBN10 1-55028-926-8
ISBN13 978-1-55028-926-8

More books in the Degrassi Junior High Series...

Spike

By Loretta Castellarin and Ken Roberts

Spike is fourteen years old-and pregnant. After one mistake at a wild party, she now faces hard decisions and questions from her boyfriend, her mother, the school, and even her friends. It's not easy, but Spike is no quitter, as she demonstrates in this stirring novelization of one of the most controversial and important storylines ever shown on Canadian television.

$9.95

ISBN10 1-55028-925-X
ISBN13 978-1-55028-925-1

MEMBER OF SCABRINI GROUP

Québec, Canada
2006